BUILD

UNIVERSES

Kit Dando

Welcome to the Bells

ISBN 9791220144490
First edition: November 2023

Welcome to the Bells

"To everyone I met along the way.
Who shared the trauma and inspired these stories."

Welcome to the Bells

Volume 1

"Hospitality is making your guests feel at home, even when you wish they were."

"How can I help you?" an unnaturally happy woman with an iPad in hand, approached Josh as he stood uncomfortably at the pub door. He wiped his clammy hand on the trousers his mum had ironed ready for a handshake.

"I'm Josh. I spoke to Josie about a trial shift." He stuttered whilst clearing his throat and holding his hand out a little too eagerly.

"Josh!" her smile grew even larger and took his hand firmly. As soon as her palm was in his, his own wrist went limp. Pulling it away quickly he smiled nervously.

Fucked the handshake, even after all the practice.

He thought to himself, but the woman didn't seem to notice or if she did, she didn't seem to care. "I'm Josie, the general manager. Follow me, we will get you settled." She turned and started to walk away. Josie was a colourful woman, long ginger hair even in a ponytail it fell past her hips. The pastel blue floral almost floor length skirt seemed to distract entirely from the fact her dull white shirt had seen happier days.

Josh followed her out of the doorway and into the pub. It was a cosy pub, even though it was mid-summer and had no business being cosy. A long bar took up the majority of the left wall, and bar tables of varying sizes were scattered around the front, each with mismatched chairs, complete with cushions of every pattern imaginable. There was a comfortable buzz of drinkers. Office workers with no blazers and loose ties, enjoying a quick pint before heading home. Middle aged women progressing through bottles of pale rosé. A couple in the corner looking to be in mid-argument whilst their child played on an iPad, a bottle of coke and packet of crisps next to him, the true taste of neglect.

Halfway across the room it was like stepping through some sort of portal entering a different dimension. It was an empty restaurant. Laid perfectly with so much glass and silverware there was no space for food. Josh looked behind him. Just to make sure he was definitely in the same place and hadn't glitched into a parallel universe. If he were in a parallel universe, he hoped he would have been doing something more interesting than a trial shift for a position as a waiter.

"This is your first job, yes?" Josie asked over her shoulder as they approached the top end of the bar. "Yes, first job."
"You are 18?"
"Yes, 18."

The end of the bar curved round, right behind it was a large dull stainless-steel lift where food was sent up, above that two rails with one ticket attached at the end that read rosemary fries. To the right of the dispense section Josh could see a waiters station with a till, some cupboards and a coffee machine which was obscured from the view of the restaurant with a small wooden wall and odd bubbly glass paneling.

"Abbie?" Josie called.

"What?" A girl called from the coffee machine as it loudly spat out hot black espresso.

"This is Josh. He's come for a trial shift. I need you to show him around." Josie didn't wait for a response and sauntered back off to the door already scrolling through a long list on her iPad.

Josh waited uncomfortably as the machine continued slowly to cough out coffee into a tall mug. Josh blew out his breath and glanced around. The girl still hadn't bothered to say a word to him but stayed invested in her caffeine. He could see she was a curvy girl wearing a checked flannel shirt and loose jeans. He suddenly felt very overdressed in his black trousers, white shirt and dad's belt. He swiftly undid a button to appear more casual just in time for her to finally turn around. Now she faced him he could see her shirt almost covered up a ketchup stain that had been poorly wiped off. Her hair looked intentionally unbrushed as it sat on her head in a brown bird's nest of a bun, but despite the almost pitiful appearance she held herself with a swagger that was intimidating even in silence.

"You worked in hospitality before?" She asked and he shook his head quickly. She took a quick gulp of her coffee before sucking in her breath. "Well, I'm Abigail, Abbie, Abs, Gail, Big G, Oi. Call me whatever you like really. I'm the head waitress. That's Eddie behind the bar." She nodded in the direction of a well-dressed man in a shirt and waistcoat, straightening his tie in the mirrored wall behind the spirit bottles. Josh suddenly felt very confused about the dress code, wondering which one of them hadn't got the memo. He didn't have long to ponder as Abbie suddenly downed her coffee, slamming the cup on the end of the bar like a shot glass, and started walking away. Josh waited a beat before understanding he needed to follow.

They walked to the back of the restaurant, passed a row of deep brown wooden tables, all looking immaculate, silver wear sparkling, glasses waiting to be filled and orbs of oil lamps waiting to be lit. Josh trotted behind Abbie who walked fast and with purpose as they made their way down a spiral staircase which was ever so slightly uneven on the last step which felt like a recipe for disaster for anyone over two pints in. They started down a corridor, toilets on the left and wooden door with STAFF ONLY at the end.

There was a fast-thumping overhead and Abbie turned fast using her forearm to push the both of them against the wall just in time for a girl to sprint past them screaming sorry like a siren as she went.

"That's Ali." Abbie introduced the blur of a human he had just seen.

They pushed through the unnaturally heavy staff door into a shorter corridor with dirty white walls and spare chairs cluttering the space. The girl tumbled out of a door on their left. Shouting fuck as she fell, running back passed them without even a quick glance at Josh.

"That's where the lockers are." Abbie gestured lazily to the door Ali had fallen out of. "And this is the office." She pointed at a dirty white door next to it, with a fist sized hole where the handle should be. She knocked but didn't wait for a response before opening it. The room inside was small, pin boards packed with papers covered every wall, a safe and printer in one corner and a computer on a desk in the other. A lanky man too tall for the chair was slumped napping in an awkward position that made Josh's back hurt just looking at him.

"That's Danny. He's the assistant manager."

She slammed the door hard behind her which was swiftly followed by a series of curses. They had continued down the corridor as the lanky boy hurried out the office whilst smoothing down his shirt.

The end of the corridor separated out in two ways.

"Kitchen." Abbie said quickly whilst pointing right and opening the door to the left. "And this is the Cellar."

Josh peered into the dark room. Towers made of crates of tonics and wines lined the room, the floor littered with beer kegs whilst the far wall held a shelf of spirits. A small hum of a fan filled the otherwise peaceful space.

"This is a good place to cry if you need to." She added helpfully, giving him a sideway glance and cocking one eyebrow. "Oh, that's Jackson." she nodded at the hooded figure in the corner Josh hadn't even noticed by the spirit bottles. Upon hearing their name, they looked over their shoulder at them. Under the black hoodie Jacksons deep Auburn hair spilled almost in front of their face, making their already pale skin look ghostly. A small knife in their hand flipped out from the end of a bottle opener, it was tiny and almost definitely blunt, but Josh took a step back anyway. Jackson raised a pair of thick dark eyebrows before returning to slicing up boxes with worrying efficiency.

They left the cellar and decided to briefly poke their heads into the kitchen. The kitchen was quiet, stock pots bubbling, knives pounding on chopping boards and Mariah Carey assuring them miracles can happen from a speaker on the large metal pass just off to the left of the door.

"All the food gets sent up via that lift in the corner so the only time you need to come in here is to get milk from the fridge. But it locks from the outside so be careful." Abbie carried on talking as they walked away. "Best not to bother the chefs. Stay up on the floor where there are witnesses." she called over her shoulder to him.
"Huh?" Josh asked, scared as he trotted behind her.
"Where there are waitresses." she repeated. "Do you smoke?"
"No never."
"You might wanna start. Only way you'll get a break."

Back upstairs, it was slowly filling up. The drinking crowd was getting heavier and younger. Danny was by the door talking to Josie whilst staring intently at the iPad. Ali was all in a fluster wandering round the restaurant looking for purpose, whilst Eddie and Jackson were behind the bar polishing glasses... *did Jackson pass us on the way up...?*

"Remember to ask tables about food allergies, don't put through stupid orders and any food that's left by the till near the coffee machine is a free for all if you are hungry. Looks like that's everything." Abbie said, looking at him for what felt like the first time. "Welcome to The Bells!"

Josh hardly had a moment to take it all in before a large chef pushed past him on a warpath for the end of the bar. Everyone quickly gathered and Josh took it as a cue to do the same.

"OK briefing time." The chef spoke quickly. He was tall and completely bald; his chin was shadowed by wisps of a beard trying to push through. His eyes were a soft blue, and his lashes were long, which made it hard to guess his age. His chef whites were a little too white but as he handed out the thick card menus still warm from the printer Josh could see his hands littered with healed burns and healing cuts. "Menu hasn't changed much. Parfit is off because dickweed forgot to make brioche, but we have a tostada I've been waiting to throw on instead, so special that at seven pounds. It's yellow tail tostada - who the fuck are you?" The chef stopped noticing Josh for the first time despite him standing next to him. Josh went to open his mouth whilst beginning to move his hand out for a handshake but was cut off. "Don't tell me, I'll learn your name if you last a week." He shook his head. "Jose what's the bookings?" he looked over to Josie who stood on the other side of him.

"We are on sixty-five so far."
"Ok not that busy so no excuses for being morons." He slammed the rest of the thick stack of menus on the end of the bar. "Let's have a good service. See you on the other side." He finished disappearing down the stairs before anyone had a chance to speak.

"OK people." Josie smiled as if it was her job to be the Doctor Jekyll to the head chef Mr. Hyde. "Usual positions. Abbie, I want you on the front with bar tables. Ali, you running the restaurant with Josh. Obviously Jacks and Ed are on bar. Dan you are on food dispense and I will be on the door." Josie nodded to everyone before strolling back off to more important things. Ali hurried after her.

"Didn't catch a word of that." Danny shrugged at Abbie. He was very tall, perhaps only an inch taller than the chef, which Josh was sure must have been a frustration for the chef. Danny also seemed to have received a different dress code to the rest of them with grey jeans the ends of which hardly skimmed his ankles, and multi coloured shirt with a geometric pattern Josh couldn't decide if it was jazzy or offensive.

"60 odd bookings. No parfit." Abbie yawned whilst scratching her scalp causing a couple more strands of hair to escape her bun.

"I am hanging so far out my arse." Danny groaned, running his hand through his blond hair, slightly matted with product.

"Bloody Baby."

"How are you upright?"

"Somewhere between 6-10 shots of espresso… I lost count." Abbie shrugged casually.

"Jesus you are going to die young." He laughed whilst walking round the other side of the bar to his battle station in front of the lift, in doing so and finally noticing Josh. "Sorry mate." He suddenly plastered on a grin. "I'm Danny."

"I'm Josh." He smiled back, a large, forced smile. *Stop, you look like a psycho.* Then his face fell a little too fast and he panicked trying to find a not creepy middle ground of a smile. "Is there something I can do?"

"I'd say your best bet is to speak to Ali. You'll be working with her." Danny smiled kindly; his light blue eyes were comforting. Josh nodded before scurrying away out of earshot. "I'd give him a week."

"Generous." Abbie huffed. "I wouldn't give him till the end of the night."

"Well as Emily Dickinson said, Hope is a thing with feathers." Danny recited watching Josh walk into a table. "What's that supposed to mean?"

"Fuck me if I know."

Ali was tapping away at the till on the far side of the restaurant when Josh approached. "Hi I'm Josh. I was told to ask you for a job." Josh spoke whilst approaching. The girl looked as if she glitched. Her head jerked to look at him and then back to the till. Her long dark blond hair was pulled back tightly into a ponytail, a thick fringe skimmed the top of her thick round glasses which were reflecting the long drink order she was tapping away. Ali seemed to be dressed for a heist, opting for an attire of full black. Black tight jeans tucked into black boots and a loose black T-shirt.

"Not much to do until bookings arrive." She muttered, going back to whispering under her breath as if muttering some sort of incantation. Josh watched her for a moment before speaking again.

"Are you ok?" he asked sincerely, and Ali let out a small laugh as if he had just asked if the Earth were round.
"Yes... no... but yes... I have my dissertation due next week and I can't even... hahaha that's funny can't even because it's on Kant. Love that for me." She laughed to herself, flicking her hair out her eyes. "And I'm working all weekend which is good but also, I don't know... but no... I mean yes, I'm fine."

She stopped speaking but Josh could tell the conversation had continued in her mind.

"Alex?" he asked, and she snapped back into the present. Her face was confused before easing out into only slightly less confusion sprinkled with exhaustion.
"Sorry erm maybe go ask Eddie if he needs anything for the bar before service starts." She turned away from the till and nodded toward the bar.

"Thank you." Josh mumbled whilst slowly heading to the bar. He felt like a pin ball being bounced about with no direction, just waiting for the slope he was on to inevitably push him into an abyss.

He approached the bar apprehensively. Jackson's eyes seemed to follow him as he got closer, but they didn't make a move past polishing the glasses. The bar was huge, taking up a large portion of the left wall, just before the end of it was a silver door within the wall where Josh could make an educated guess where the food came up, trailing off from that was the waitress station. Just before the food lift was a doorway through which Josh could see a small room with a dishwasher and a collection of different coloured bins. The view in front of him was spectacular, the lower half of the back wall was taken up by a large mirror which reflected the entire restaurant, the top half was filled with shelves at uneven heights. Each shelf promoted a different alcohol, fancy gins, whiskeys and vodkas. The top shelf was stacked with impressive magnums of red wine. Each display was linked with vines and flowers trailing, falling and flowing down just touching the tips of the spirits lined up precisely in front of the mirror. Josh caught his reflection for a moment, his curly brown hair was already flicking down in front of his right eye, his pale complexion already looking clammy with nerves.

The bartender, Eddie, looked as if he had also walked into the wrong building. He wore almost a three-piece suit, crisp white shirt with a burgundy waistcoat and matching tie. His dark black hair was neatly combed to one side.

"Erm, I'm Josh. I'm new and looking for something to help with." Josh tried to sound confident, but he already hated the sound of his own voice and name.

Eddie turned around and looked at him with raised eyebrows, then over to Jackson who shrugged before his eyes rested back with Josh. He looked intelligent, in his early thirties and already fed up with the newbie in front of him. "Can I help?" Josh pushed for an answer.

"parlo inglese ma non lo farò ma questo è davvero un grande scherzo." *Of course.* Josh sighed. "È un'idea di Danny, scusate." He carried on. Josh picked up the name Danny and nodded quickly before running back to Danny who was still at the end of the bar.

"What can I do?" Josh felt exhausted just at the prospect of finding something to do.

"Well, you got a table in your section to maybe start with that." He nodded at two people sitting at the far end of the restaurant. Josh turned to see two middle aged women, already sipping gin. He turned back to Danny who was holding out a couple of menus with a cheeky grin slapped on his face.

"My section?" he asked, his stomach felt like stone butterflies were causing havoc inside it. "I'm not sure."

"As Salena Godden said, Courage is a muscle." Danny grinned again. "They won't bite." He turned away before Josh could gleam any more support from his new colleague.

Josh cautiously approached the table and forced a smile.

"Hi, I'm Josh and I'll be your server today." He started placing menus down. *Shouldn't have given a name. They'll know exactly who to name in the review when it all goes wrong.* "We have run out of parfit but have a tostada on special today." *Well done Josh. You remembered the briefing. You'll get on the good side of the chefs. Good start.* "Can I get you some water?" *This is easy. Just smile and wave. Just smile and wave.*

The lady smiled and looked up at him. "What is Tostada?"

He gulped. *Bollocks!*

7:00pm

Only an hour into the shift Josh felt like a fish out of water.

"Josh, where are the drinks for table 69?" Abbie asked quickly. Josh spun round looking across the room whilst counting round to find which was 69. The system was ridiculous jumping from 15 to 50 to 107. It was as if a toddler who had just learnt numbers had assigned them all. A toddler may have done a better job. He lost count twice before Abbie rolled her eyes and walked away. He ran to the bar and waved to Eddie who was elegantly pouring tonics into tall glasses with one hand and shaking a cocktail with the other.
"Are those for table 69?" he asked desperately.
"Non c'è un tavolo sessantanove." Eddie raised his shoulders in surrender. Josh took a deep breath wishing he had taken Italian over French for his GCSE's.

7:37pm

"Excuse me Sir. Can I get you another drink?" Josh smiled gesturing to the empty glass in front of the lone man. Josh was determined to leave the shift where no one could say he didn't try. The man had been sat in the bar area on a small table for two tucked away in the corner. He was holding a newspaper but was evidently not reading it since it was upside down. Originally Josh had assumed he was waiting for someone but as the hours passed it became evident that the man was alone. He looked as if he hadn't washed for a while and his thinning hair was strategically combed most likely to cover a bald spot.

"Hmm." The man mulled it over. "Nooopee. You can'tt but the one with theee nice arsee can." He chuckled to himself over his slurred words and Josh bit his tongue. Josh suddenly felt a bit sick and not just because the overpowering smell of tobacco and beer from the man's breath was turning his stomach. Josh backed away slowly. Not sure how to handle the situation he turned around weighing up in his mind who to go to for help. Taking a step back into the direction of the main dining area he bumped immediately into Abbie.
"What's up?" Abbie asked as she saw his expression.

"That guy over there wants to order a drink." He nodded in the direction. "I think he's already had enough."
"Oh, did he harass you?" she tutted casually. "That's just Clive. Friendly neighbourhood alcoholic." Abbie smirked. "Although he's not really friendly and He doesn't live around here. He is a misogynistic prick but spends lots of money so the owner doesn't want us to ban him. What can ya do, eh?" She shrugged it off with a laugh.
"Well he asked for the one with the nice arse." Josh's face flushed red, feeling uncomfortable even repeating it, not able to look Abbie in the eye as he spoke.
"Just send him Danny, his arse is good enough."

"Danny how do I."

"Sorry mate dealing with a fuck up. Can you ask Molly?" Danny cut him off whilst turning away and back to the lift. He was yanking tickets off of the metal rail just above it which was overflowing with orders. To the average customer in the building Danny looked busy but Josh was closer and could see it was blind panic dressed up in hard work, so he decided not to press for any more help.

Ask Molly…Who the fuck is Molly? He turned scanning the room. Josh looked around for a waitress he hadn't met. He turned back to Danny trying to cover the embarrassment on his face that he had no idea who Molly was but before he could even begin to form a question Jackson pushed past, covered in a thin brown looking liquid, it had dripped through their hair, making it look like they had shoved their face into a puddle. Josh sprang out of the way, they gave him a harsh look through narrowed eyes, whether narrowed in anger or because of the beverage seeping into them Josh couldn't tell.

"I'll find Molly." He spoke more to himself than anyone else as he backed away. The restaurant was almost full now, the last bookings were taking up the remaining empty seats. Despite it being almost full capacity, the atmosphere was calm and sophisticated. Daylight had fully disappeared which left most of the lighting down to oil lamps dotted around the tables and edge of the room. Josh quickly gave up the game of where's Molly and began hunting for Abbie. Josh made his way into the front of the pub, into the drinking area and weaved his way through a large group of office workers who were either having a very good or very, very bad week judging by the amount of alcohol they were chugging through. He approached Abbie at the far end of the bar as she was piling far too many drinks for his liking onto a tray.

"Abbie." He hissed. "Who's Molly?"

"What do you mean?" she looked at him quizzically.

"Saw her just now." She tutted and shrugged before walking away with her alcoholic balancing act. Josh watched her in a mixture of fear and awe as she approached a large group of what could only be described as 'lads' and unloaded the beers effortlessly.

He continued to scan the room for anyone who looked like they were working, anyone moving fast and with purpose.

Josh ran over to Ali, intercepting her as she made her way back over to the dispense section arms loaded with dirty plates.

"Erm excuse me." He asked, feeling slightly embarrassed. "Where's Molly?"

"hmm she was just here…" She took a moment to look around. "Must have gone to the loo or something..." she shrugged and carried on her journey to drop off the plates.

He turned back to the bustling restaurant.

Who the fuck is Molly?

8:56pm

"You can do this. You can do this." Josh muttered to himself as he paced the small corridor. "They are just people.

Like you." He took another breath. His hands were shaking, and he could feel the sweat seeping through his shirt. "Just do it."

Bursting into the kitchen before he could change his mind. All confidence vanished as five chefs stopped in their tracks to stare at him entering their territory. He felt like a gazelle who had walked into a lion's den to ask for directions.

"Yes?" The head chef who had been upstairs before asked, already sounding fed up. He was working on the side of the pass closest to the door, plating up food Josh had spent the whole night mispronouncing.
"I've been sent down to ask how long the wait is on table 69?" he said as bravely as he could. The head chef pinched his nose with thumb and forefinger and took a deep breath.
"Tell Danny I have cucumbers in the fridge he can fuck himself with."

9:05pm

Josh logged onto the till by the dispense section, starting his search among the buttons of wine, the customer's pronunciation sounded like a Frenchman with something stuck in his throat but after asking him for the third time to repeat himself, the social law dictated he must smile, nod and leave. "Erm Danny?" Josh asked over his shoulder, remembering one of the tables further requests "Do you know where I can find a decanter? That table in the corner wants one."
"Erm, have you tried under the sofa?" he offered.

Sofa? He must have meant the ridiculously long deep purple thing under one of the windows of the drinking section.

"Might be in the kitchen?"
Josh took a deep breath not looking forward to going back into the chef's lair.
"Could it be in the bloody fridge for all I know." he sighed frustrated.
"It's ok." Josh called back to him. "I'm sure I'll find it."

Josh finally settled on clicking on a button with a wine that sounded fancy but also wouldn't be found too close to the bottom of the menu.

"I don't know babe." *Babe?*

Josh turned abruptly, not sure how his relationship with the assistant manager had progressed so fast.

"Love you too." Danny finished before hanging up the phone in his hand. He noticed Josh staring. "Girlfriend can't find the Tv remote." he rolled his eyes.
"Where can I find a decanter?" Josh asked. Danny reached up to the top of the cupboards pulling one down.
"Thanks."

10:20pm

"Abbie, I'm really sorry to bother you again but table 4 said they didn't order these fries." Josh explained, completely exasperated.
"Oh dear!" she tutted whilst helping herself to one and moving it next to the till by three other portions of chips which had been almost completely devoured by staff.

Josh ran a hand through his hair and dropped his head onto the bar. He groaned aloud.

"So how do you feel to be near the end of your worst shift?"
"Huh?" his head sprung up.
"Your first shift?" she repeated herself with a suspicious smile. Most of the restaurant was empty now, a few couples dotted about having late dinners. The drinking crowd was still alive but not demanding much attention.

"I'm going for a smoke." she announced, shoving another handful of chips in her mouth before almost skipping outside.

"Josh." Ali called whilst pounding up the stairs. Josh looked over his shoulder wearily.
"Yes?"

"Josie wants to see you in the office." Josh's stomach dropped.

Josh slowly walked to the office, taking each step down the spiral staircase mournfully as if they were going to be his last.

You've done nothing wrong... actually you've done everything wrong, but it was your first shift... they can't fire you... well you don't have the job yet; you can't be fired from a job you don't even have. Except maybe you really were that bad and you are going to be the first person to lose a job you don't have.

Josh knocked on the office door and Josie pulled it open all too fast, still smiling. *Surely, she can't still be happy.*

"Josh!" She greeted him with the same enthusiasm she had at the beginning of the shift.
"You wanted to see me?"

Danny was cackling in the office chair at something on the computer with the head chef and a tall female chef Josh had yet to meet. They were all laughing at something on the CCTV footage and Josh suddenly felt very self-conscious.

"Dan, watch Jackson get covered in espresso martini another time. Everyone out please" The three of them shuffled out still giggling.

Josie stepped aside so he could enter. She cleared a stack of paper off a chair and gestured Josh to sit whilst dumping into on top of another stack of paper which sat next to another stack of papers. She plonked herself down on the precarious office chair Danny had recently vacated and beamed at Josh.

"So" She started. "How do you think it went?"

So badly.

"Yeah, fine, yeah." He muttered.
"You did great from what I could see!"

She must be blind.

"Thank you."

"What would your availability be like? Are you looking for part-time or full-time hours?"
or maybe no hours…

"Well, I want to save some money before uni, I'm not sure how much is a good amount to put away, but maybe..." *she didn't ask for your life story.* "Probably somewhere in-between."

"Ok lovely well that works with us!" she smiled even more. "Well, I would love to offer you the job, so if you would like to take it just let me know by Saturday so if you will join us, I can add you to the rota when I make it on Sunday."
"So tomorrow?"
"It's Saturday tomorrow?" her eyes glazed over suddenly and for a short flickering moment she stopped smiling. "Thank you for letting me know." She smiled again but this time there was evident effort, and Josh wasn't sure whether to leave her to the crisis beginning behind her eyes.

"Thank you for today." He spoke to interrupt whatever cogs had malfunctioned in her mind.

"Thank you. Feel free to stay and have a pint before you go." The thought of a beer made his whole body jerk with a new found lease for life. "If you wouldn't mind popping into the kitchen and sending Scott to me if he is there." Josh looked quizzically. "Scott is the head chef." Josh nodded and left the office, careful not to trip over the folders and papers.

He wandered down the short corridor and poked his head into the kitchen. Everything was off and quiet. The floor still glistened slightly from having been recently mopped. He wandered in feeling safer to enter now. The pass, the main stoves, grill and pot washing section took up the entire space which was visible from glancing through the door but moving in further and looking around the corner was like peeking into the Tardis. The room stretched out further than he could have imagined, lines of counters, pots and pans piled on shelves, more stoves and another sink. The quiet felt out of place here. It felt like he was standing in a physical oxymoron.

The sound of a door opening interrupted the first bit of peace Josh had felt since he arrived. Josh hurried back round the corner feeling like a child caught sneaking in the kitchen at night looking for sweets.

"Can I help?" Scott asked as he appeared out of the walk-in fridge. Still in his chef whites with some paper in his hand he looked tired and with no time to waste on the new boy.
"Josie wants you." He spoke fast and scared. Scott said nothing but immediately left to go to the office.

He blew out a breath and turned to leave. He started toward the door, but his eye was caught by a white board which hung next to the fridge. He wouldn't have seen it without entering the kitchen fully. One half of it was covered in notes, order sheets and menus, whilst the other side made Josh's heart sink.

Newbie bets

Danny – 1 week

Eddie - 1 week

Tom – 3 weeks

Chris – 1 ½ weeks

Molly – 2 weeks

Matteo – 4 weeks

Abbie – 1 day

Perhaps it was a blessing his mood didn't have far to fall. He blew out his breath feeling almost embarrassed. Not sure if he was more hurt by the fact that they were betting against him or that Abbie might be right. The longest bet was four weeks.

Only four weeks. They had so little faith.

Four weeks wasn't very long, when he thought about it. He could do four weeks. Four weeks was just 28 days, only 20 working days. 20 days is nothing. Four weeks. He could do it.

Josh left the kitchen fresh with purpose. To say a fire had lit inside him would be a massive over statement but something had caught alight, it might have resembled a small flame of a scented candle, but it was a spark none-theless.

With a grin on his face, he knocked on the office door abruptly before he changed his mind.

"Come in." Josie called.

"I'll take the job." He announced proudly before he had fully opened the door.
"Amazing!" Josie beamed at him. Josh stood there for a beat, Josie and Scott staring at him expectantly. He forced a large smile before nodding to them both and closing the door. *Far too dramatic.*

Lost in his own embarrassment he immediately found himself colliding into a chef coming out of the staff area. He looked to be just past his mid-twenties, dark short hair, evident if he grew it out anymore it would form tight small curls, his thin face was lightly tanned, he looked tired but with a smile of a day well spent.

"Sorry" Josh stuttered out quickly.
"No worries." He grinned. "So, you staying?" he asked with a little too much interest. Josh could immediately place his Italian accent and wondered how much he had bet.
"Yeah I think I will stick around." Josh replied as they climbed the stairs together.
"Good answer." The boy winked. "Tough shift?"
"I think so. Not much to compare it to." He chuckled as they climbed the stairs together.

The restaurant was empty now, a few drinkers hanging back already too drunk to care what the staff were doing.

"What did you bunch of bastards put the poor sod through?" The boy shouted to the front of house team as he took a seat at the bar, a cold amber coloured pint already waiting before he had even decided where he was going to sit.

"He did good." Eddie smiled whilst wrapping pots of fruit in cling film. Josh smiled for a moment, happy for a word of encouragement, but his smile faded as fast as it arrived when he realised it was in English.

It was all a joke.

He wasn't sure whether he wanted to laugh or cry. Or do both… his CV had said he was a multitasker.

Eddie put a pint down next to the chef and gestured for Josh to sit down.

"So… it was all a joke?" Josh said aloud, still processing it.
"Most likely." The chef laughed while taking a sip.
"All the random fries?"
"Probably Abbie."

"69?" Josh asked.
"Only in the bedroom."
"Molly is probably made up too."
"No Molly is real." The chef laughed and turned around. "Mols!" he waved at Ali, who was laying up the restaurant. "Ali is short for Aioli. Long story." *Don't ask.* "But the nickname stuck."
Josh gulped down half his pint.
"I'm Matt by the way. Well, it's actually Matteo, and really Matteo is actually my middle name, but Matt or Mattie is fine. I'm the larder chef."
"I'm Josh and I'm a gullible twat." Matt laughed whilst

choking down his beer.

"Don't stress, it's happened to all of us. You should have seen Ali at the end of her trial shift."

Abbie walked over with a handful of fries. "You stayin' then?" she asked, Josh couldn't read her expression but nodded whilst taking a gulp of beer.

"Better pay up Abs." Matt smirked and slapped the top of the bar.

"Nah Nah he hasn't rocked up to his second shift yet, I still got time." She narrowed her eyes at him.

"What do you win?" Josh asked curiously.

"We all put a fiver in, and you win the pot, plus 1 drink of your choice paid for by the losers." Josh nodded slowly in approval. "If you make it four weeks, I win, you get my drink." Matt held out his hand.

"You got a deal." Josh shook it firmly. *Handshake practice paying off now.*

Josh grinned at Abbie feeling like he had finally made a worthy move.

She grinned, patted his shoulder and turned away.

"Welcome to hell."

"What?" Josh asked, suddenly nervous.

"Welcome to the bells."

Welcome to the Bells

Volume 2

Fuck. Fuck. Fuck. Late again.

Despite what Ali had put in her cover letter she was not the best at time management. After a long day of lectures, followed by a long night of writing essays, followed by another long day of seminars and tutorials about next steps after graduating, Ali was ready to clock out even before she had clocked in. She could have started her essay earlier. Maybe if she hadn't gone out drinking with Abbie on Monday and worked instead... Ali thought back to her studies on Charles Darwin in second year. 'A man who dares to waste an hour of time has not discovered the value of life'... Ali was sure Charles Darwin never ran out of Yorkshire puddings whilst working short staffed in a restaurant on a Sunday Lunch. Monday was a necessity for her own sanity. And after all was it not Bertrand Russel who said, 'The time you enjoy wasting is not wasted time'? *Why am I doing a degree in contradictions?*

Ali pounded down the street to The Bells.

"I know. I'm sorry!" She shouted as she ran past Josie at the door. Josie rolled her eyes without looking up from her iPad. She trotted through the pub as fast as she could without causing too much of a commotion. Taking the stairs two at a time she tripped over the last one to be caught by Mattie, whose hair was damp with sweat, his chef whites seasoned with speckles of sauces.

"You ok?" he asked.
"Late!" She was all her brain could manage as she pulled herself up and continued down the poorly lit corridor into the staff area. She threw her bag into the staff room before pelting back up the stairs.

Ali pushed two pens in her ponytail and tucked another two in her back pocket. Two half-finished notepads were shoved into the pouch of her pinny, after tying it firmly around her waist she lopped a bottle opener into the band. Fully armed for service she allowed herself to take a breath and survey the battlefield.

Only two tables in the restaurant were in use, clearly people loitering from lunch. Their tables were very empty and most likely their lives if they could afford to watch the froth from an hour old cappuccino dry into a crust. The drinkers were a normal crowd of people who looked as if they had just come from a meeting so important it would pop into your inbox with a red marker on it, but these same people were also already drunk and despite Ali being late it still wasn't yet six o'clock.

A man at the end of the bar waved at Ali. instinctively she waved back, but she knew she had no idea who he was. He looked confused, so she let her hand drop to her side and checked behind in case he was waving to someone else but only the coffee machine and the collection of different coloured metallic water bottles for the staff was sharing the waitress station with her. He raised his empty pint glass, and she exhaled a deep breath in an attempt to waiver her embarrassment.

"How can I help you sir?" she plastered on the best grin she could as she walked to the end of the bar where he was sat.

"Pint of lager please love. And another bowl of peanuts." He smiled lazily; it must have been his third... at least. "Of course." She smiled whilst scooping another serving of nuts into his bowl and reaching for a pint glass.

"Long day?" he asked with a sympathetic smile. *You have no idea.* She almost laughed to herself. He leaned over a bit and lowered his voice. "Your t-shirt is inside out love." Ali paused in front of the Amstel tap and looked down, sure enough she could see a Primark label staring back at her from her plain black t-shirt. Ali let out an exhausted laugh and thanked him before pouring his pint. "So, what do you do?" he asked.

"You might be shocked to find out that I am a waitress." She joked trying to erase the tower of embarrassment that was building in front of her. To her relief he laughed.

"But come on. You've got a proper job, right?" he asked with a smile and raised eyebrows.

A proper job...Is what I'm doing not proper? What's wrong with it? People work in hospitality whilst studying. That is normal. But I'm close to graduating... oh God... I'm close to graduating. That means real life. The bubble

has popped. The safety net, gone. My student loan, gone.
My decisions have consequences. Picking mould off food
will no longer be socially acceptable. What do I do? My
back hurts thinking about it all. Fuck. I'll have to pay
council tax. What do I do? Get a proper job… but this is
a proper job… isn't it? It comes with paychecks, training
days and bad habits of emotional suppression… what
isn't proper about that?

"Ah!" Eddie's distressed shriek knocked Ali out of her internal debate. She hadn't noticed the waterfall of lager that had been steadily flowing and collecting in a puddle by her feet.

"I'm sorry." She floundered and looked around for a blue roll in a panic.
"Get out!" Eddie waved his hand dismissively. "There is no waste behind my bar… except my talent." Eddie flicked his head, a strand of black hair escaping from its perfect positioning. Ali shuffled around Eddie bumping into Jackson who had apparated with a mop, she ran downstairs to put her shirt the right way round and continue to internally debate her place in society.

Jackson finished cleaning up the mess and Eddie finished overacting in time as Scott came up for briefing. Josie didn't join them at the end of the bar but stayed at the front door. Scott smiled at them all but the agitation behind his grin was evident.

"Ok ladies, gents, and Abbie." Scott started whilst Abbie looked quizzical trying to work out if she had been insulted or not. "Today should be an easy shift, no changes, no specials. As simple as Dan." Danny smiled briefly before joining Abbie in a confused offence.

"I checked, and we only have 40 booked so sounds like we have a nice evening on our hands."

He was interrupted by Matt hastily making his way over. "Ali is having an existential crisis in the walk-in fridge. Can one of you come get her?" He looked round at the front of house team. Abbie put down her coffee and made her way downstairs.

Scott sighed "I jinxed it." He took a deep breath before giving them all one last glare and departing.

Eddie and Jackson shuffled off back to prepping for the evening. Danny stayed in a thoughtful gaze at his position in dispense.

"How strange…" Danny spoke to himself.

"What?" Josh asked and Danny jumped a little forgetting he was next to him.

"Josie didn't join us for the briefing." he explained, and Josh joined him staring at Josie standing by the open door, forever tapping away at her iPad.

"She probably knows everything anyway though." Josh shrugged.

"Of course she does but she says its principal. One team, One dream and all that jazz."

Josie turned around as if sensing they were both looking at her. She made her way over to them, with a big smile.

"Ok you two!" Josie smiled warmly. "Josh I would like to put you on the drinks section tonight, help you get used to the alcohol side of the menu." Josie pushed her smile even wider before walking away.

Josh and Danny turned to each other shrugging in sync. Josh walked away with a small grin feeling like he had made a small connection with Danny even if it were just through confusion.

Danny turned to make himself a coffee, pouring the milk into a small stainless-steel jug and placing it just under the steaming wand. He watched absent minded as the white liquid started to form a little whirlpool. He could tell the milk was perfectly frothed by just the sound now, just a small hiss of air coming out from the shiny white liquid. Putting it down, he cleaned the nozzle and flipped the steamer off and on, he had forgotten why he had to do that but knew from years ago when he was first trained, he knew he was supposed to. Pouring the milk over the espresso slowly, wiggling the jug to cause white ripples is the golden brown, the perfect latte tree. He looked at it and smiled. His parents told him he was wasting his time in the pub but look he could make a perfect tree with milk... who's laughing now dad?

Danny brought the mug to his lips ready to take a sip, but it was snatched out of his hands.

"What the fuck Abs?" he cursed as she took a large gulp. She gave him a small smirk and any frustration faded. "Is Al ok?" he asked as he turned to start on another coffee. "Yeah she's fine. Just feels like her youth is sliding through her fingers."
"Don't we all?" He laughed.
"At least twice a week." Abbie agreed.

"How soon Hath time, the subtle thief of youth." Danny spoke over the steady hiss of the steamer. "John Milton." he answered the question she hadn't asked.

Danny finished making the second coffee, placing it down and beginning the quick cleaning ritual. He turned back but the coffee was gone.

"What the...?" he started before clocking Jackson sipping it a few paces away down the bar. "Come on jacks!" He sighed as they raised their eyebrows. "Yeah, you're right you do a lot for me." He conceded and began again.

Milk. Espresso. Pour. Wipe. Steam.

"Thanks Danny I really needed this today." Ali sighed, taking it from his hands as he turned around, she sipped it slowly and let out a satisfied humm of approval. "If anyone gets cut early tonight, can it be me? I just don't have it in me today." She placed the coffee on the end of the bar, looking down at the distorted tree in the foam.

"Course Al." Danny spoke as softly as he could through gritted teeth whilst staring at the coffee he should be drinking.

"You wanna talk about it?" Abbie offered whilst placing her own coffee down. Ali took a deep breath.

"I just don't see the point, you know. I know this isn't my future. But it's a means to an end. But then when does it end? How do I pursue my future when I have no time because I'm working here? I mean I could, but I'll be so burnt out. I just..." she trailed off staring into space. Abbie and Danny glanced at each other and shrugged. She snapped out of her daze and turned to her two friends. "You know?"

"We do." They said in sync.

"Ali." Josie interrupted the group therapy at the end of the bar at the end of the bar just as Danny finished making his fourth coffee. "Just sat a group of six in your section. It's a birthday party. The birthday girl is the young one wearing too much makeup." She smiled. "Aw Thank you Danny." Josie took the coffee from him and walked away before he could even process the need for protest.

"How do I look?" Ali sighed looking Abbie dead in the eyes and forced a smile. It was unnatural, too many teeth on show, cheeks puffed up uncomfortably, and eyebrows raised awkwardly.

"Try again." Abbie instructed and Ali pushed a new attempt at happiness onto her face. "You look terrifying." Abbie laughed. She pushed another smile. "Better. Go get 'em!" Abbie winked, whilst Ali yanked her ponytail tighter before heading in the direction of the loud laughter and ridiculous balloons.

Abbie watched Ali like a proud mother sending a child to school.

"You know I'll take it as a compliment." Danny spoke whilst straightening the collar on his shirt which looked more like an information pamphlet for a nature trail considering the vast array of birds on it.
"Huh?" Abbie looked at him quizzically.
"Everyone stealing my coffee. It's because I do make the best ones." He said with pride, jutting out his chin whilst flicking a fallen flop of blond hair out of his eyes and back in line where the rest of his hair sat perfectly styled.
"If you say so."
"Becca says I make great coffee." he smiled.
"She is your girlfriend. it's in the contract to be nice." She sipped her drink and looked away, watching the slow

42

trickle of customers filing into the bar and restaurant. Josh collected a couple of gin and tonics from the collection point on the other side of the bar and tried to give them to two wrong tables before finding them the right home.

"Are you saying someone makes better coffee than me?" he snorted, pulling Abbie's attention back to him.

"Yes, I do." She retorted, insulted it were even in question. "Mine are like drinking caffeinated velvet!"

"Mine are art!" he shot back fast, holding up the almost empty coffee in front of Abbie which still held a loose shape of leaves. "I could have an Instagram page for them." *I should start an Instagram page for them.*

"Don't start an Instagram page." Abbie rolled her eyes. "Ok Picasso. But looks mean nothing if the taste isn't there." She patted his shoulder.

"Well at least I'm better at my job than you." Abbie let out an attractive cackle at his statement. "What? I am better!"

"I am 100% better. No doubt about it." Abbie continued to laugh at him.

"No way I've been in this industry longer" Danny said smugly.

"I know which must make it hard to face the fact that you are inferior."

"But I am charming as fuck." Danny smoldered and Abbie grimaced and gently shoved him. "Josh." Danny shouted to grab his attention as he walked past looking lost with a pad and pen in hand. He smiled in response. "Who is better at their job out of me and Abbie?" he asked casually.

"I'll be honest I don't even know what you guys are supposed-

"Ok, thanks anyway, carry on." Danny dismissed him and Josh turned and wandered off to look lost in a different area of the pub.

"Eddie!" Abbie Hollard at him.
"What do you need?" he asked, not looking at them but staying focused on the six perfectly equal glasses of prosecco.
"Who is the best server?"
"Ali." He answered immediately and popped open another bottle of Prosecco. He threw the cork in their direction and smiled to himself as it sailed effortlessly into the bin to the side of the food lift.

"You could have at least pretended to hesitate." Danny scoffed.
Eddie looked at him "Hmmm… Ali. Happy now?" He went back to focus on his drinks.

"I mean out of me and Danny." Abbie re-phrased the question.
"If either of you ever decide to do your job, I might be able to judge but that remains to be seen." He shrugged. The two of them had locked eyes and glared. The stalemate was broken when Danny suggested a bet.

"Ok whoever gets the most tips at the end of the night is the better server." Danny proposed.
"You aren't allowed to flirt with anyone." Abbie looked at him seriously.
"And you aren't allowed to give out freebies."
"Deal." She offered her hand which he shook firmly.

"Jackson!" Danny shouted and they popped their head out of the glass washroom. "Cover dispense, I'm working the floor tonight." They looked over to Eddie for permission who rolled his eyes. Jackson shrugged and took

Danny's position in front of the lift just in time for a ticket to appear.

7:00pm

"Hello, Afternoon, how are we doing today?" Ali approached the couple who sat down in her section.
"We are good, thank you. How are you?" *On the fuckin brink.*

"I am just fantastic!" she laughed. And laughed and continued to laugh. The couple looked from her to each other sharing an awkward smile.

"Can I get you some water?" Ali asked, still laughing slightly. She didn't wait for a response before walking away in the direction of the bar, in her trance she almost walked into Abbie who was making her way to a table which contained at least three generations of one family on it, four if you included the slightly terrifying doll the younger child seemed to be mothering.

"Hello everyone!" She announced her presence loudly. "Bottle of Sanceer, pint of larger, two Coca Colas and a bowl of water for the dog!" Abbie placed the stainless-steel dog bowl by the edge of the table. The whole table began laughing when they spotted the ice floating in it and a slice of lemon and lime pushed into the edge.

"Oh, thank you!" The mother smiled.

"Got to give everyone the best experience." She smiled back sweetly.

Turning away from the table, Danny was staring at her, mouth set in a frustrated line.

"Really?" He asked, raising his eyebrows. She gave him a wink and he couldn't help one corner of his mouth flick up.

Abbie made her way to the bar to deposit the black tray back ready for the next order to be placed on it.

Josh stood at the end of the bar, eyes scanning the front whilst making notes.

"What ya looking at?" Abbie asked.
"Just wanted to make a note of all the beers, the ones in the drinks menu I think need updating." Josh spoke proudly before realising Abbie was the last person to care about initiative. "What are those ones?" Josh asked, pointing at two mystery taps with no label.
"Those are two guest ales. they change each week and sometimes they forget to send us the clips for them." She explained. "The right one is Waddle it be, And the left is Naked Ladies." she explained. Josh's pen stopped writing on the word naked and looked up confused. But Abbie was already sprinting to the door, beating Danny there by seconds, greeting and seating a young couple. She pulled out their chairs for them whilst animatedly introducing herself.

Naked Ladies... Waddle it be...

Josh looked over to Eddie as he flipped the top off a tonic with his bar blade with such force it flew into the air high enough for him to bat it straight into the bin. Josh would have been more impressed if he was less focused on the information he had just been given.

Good try Abbie. He thought to himself, crossing through those notes on his pad and straightening his shirt. *Not going to fool me this time.*

7:47pm.

"No way you can remember the whole order." The group of girls all shook their heads in disbelief as Danny recited the order in its entirety, correctly including the details of doubles, singles, light tonic, flavoured tonics, large and medium wines, cocktails with exactly the number of straws necessary.

"That is so impressive." The ringleader clapped. He felt smug as they all knew you only really needed to please each group's alpha as they would be the ones calculating the bill including calculating the tip.

"Thank you. I am here all week" Danny graciously bowed. "Actually, not Mondays or Wednesdays." he corrected, and they all erupted in laughter whilst Danny briefly considered a career in stand-up he clocked Abbie watching with a smirk of frustration on her face.

"Could we add a couple of portions of olives onto the order?" One girl with fake eyelashes so thick Danny wasn't entirely sure she could see him from underneath them.

"Of course. Garlic or Spanish trio?"

Garlic or Spanish Trio? Josh overheard as he wandered in the direction of the till with a simple order of two martinis written on his notepad.

"Josh mate, can you do me a favour?" Matteo asked as appeared up the stairs. Some customers looked on in slight awe as they saw a chef in full whites, in the restaurant before them, as the realisation that real people had to deal with their orders of deconstructed burgers was made apparent before their eyes.

"What do you need?" Josh asked with a smile, knowing full well already that he probably couldn't help but didn't want to lose the faith of the only person who had his back. "Normally I'd ask Josie, but she and Scott had…" he broke off waving it off. "Not important but could you pop to the bakery round the corner as we have run out of Hoagie rolls." Matteo looked about impatiently. Josh looked at him quizzically as his brain processed the request slower than a 2005 dell laptop.

Hoagie rolls? What a ridiculous name. They could at least invent something more realistic.

Josh smirked and rolled his eyes.

"Hoagie rolls?" He scoffed. "And I thought you were on my side Matt." He tutted with disappointment and walked away.

Matt stood confused at the end of the bar and looked over to Eddie who sighed, both more used to working with children than Maria Von Trapp.

Eddie looked over to Jacks as they spiked a ticket before moving back to polishing glasses. Performing two jobs without breaking a sweat despite both being constantly exposed to hot food or steamy glasswashers.

"Zanahoria?" He called and they made their way over. "What's going on with Josie?" He asked, jutting his chin in their manager's direction as she laughed with a couple of local barristers who never say no to dessert wine.

Jackson nodded in the direction of the stairs.

"But Scott and Josie never fight." He gasped whilst Jackson pushed their eyebrows up and grimaced. "That bad? hmm. We'll burn that bridge when we come to it." Jackson decided not to correct him as the methodic ticking of a printing ticket began behind him, he loosened his emerald tie slightly and sighed deeply. "Lord have mercy."

8:33pm.

"I'm not sure what I am doing anymore." Ali spoke quickly, not even trying to force a smile.
"I thought you were coming to take our order?" The middle-aged gentleman looked up to her, his dainty glasses balanced on the tip of his nose, the wine menu open in his hand, his finger already poised over the Montepulciano he was probably going to pronounce incorrectly.
"Is that what I'll be doing for the rest of my life? Just taking orders... most likely from men less qualified than me... is that really…

"It's the Montepulciano you want, is it sir?" Abbie's bright voice barged into the conversation as she apparated behind Ali steering her out the way. "Can I get you anything else?" Her voice raised a few decibels higher, whilst her cheek muscles began to tremble from their unexpected work out today. Abbie removed the standard wine glasses, ready to be replaced with larger red ones, she pushed them into Ali's hands who was still standing next to her in an existential trance.

"We would love some of that soda bread and whipped butter." He smiled back, removing his glasses and tucking them into his blazer, Abbie took the wine menu away whilst achieving the impossible of pushing her smile even wider. Turning abruptly, she manoeuvred Ali through the restaurant toward the front of the bar.

"Do you need to take five Al?" Abbie asked quickly but kindly. She took the wine glasses from her hand passing them to Jackson who was ready to receive them on the other side of the bar. "It's ok if you do." She continued pulling the pad and pen out her hand and tucking them into Ali's pinny. "I can cover your section." She finished pushing Ali's glasses back up her nose and straightening her shirt.

"Would you mind?" Ali finally broke from her trance. "I think I need chamomile tea."

As Ali shuffled off to the coffee machine Abbie turned back round to the restaurant, catching Danny walking an elderly woman out the door into a black cab which waited out front. The lady gave his cheek a squeeze before squeezing a note into his hand.

Danny swaggered back inside bringing an air of confidence. He sauntered over to Abbie flashing her a quick look at the £20 before pushing it into his back pocket.

"Thought I said no flirting." she raised her eyebrows with a smirk.

Danny slouched against the edge of the bar, bringing himself a little closer to Abbies height. "She's not my type."

"What? Mature?" Danny gave her a light shove. "Hope you know you've stolen her grandkids birthday money."

"One of you." Josie approached them; her normally happy tone had been cut short and it caught them both off guard.

"Are you alright?" Danny asked sincerely, concerned at what had temporarily broken through Josie's spell of joy.

"Yes, fine thank you." she pushed a smile back onto her face, but it was evidently forced and frustrated. "There has been a mistake with table two's order, and I need you to go and tell Scott we need another tartar sent up. I just don't want to deal with him tonight and would really appreciate it if you could."

"You guys ok...?" Abbie probed carefully.

"Just a disagreement that's all."

"Never mind what the haters say, ignore them till they fade away." Danny wisely quoted T.I. Josie nodded a thank you, her face crinkled up in confusion as she turned away in a flurry of floral skirt.

"What do you think that is about?" Abbie asked.

"Ah. I'm sure whatever it is will blow over." He shrugged it off whilst heading to the kitchen, preparing to get shouted at.

8:54pm.

"Hi guys, just wanted to come back over and see if I can get you any more drinks?" Josh approached two ladies who had been sitting in a quiet corner slowly progressing through a bottle of Sauvignon Blanc, the New Zealand one, not the French of course.

"We were actually just wondering if you were still

running those duck doughnut bar snacks you were mid-week?" one of the ladies answered, she sounded as if she had strolled right off the set of Downtown Abby and held her wine glass so high it must be giving her arm ache.
Duck doughnuts? Is that savoury or sweet? Sounds disgusting either way.

"Duck doughnuts?" Josh said slowly testing the words out. "You know what let me check." He smiled as politely as he could and turned on his heels. He scanned the room looking for Ali who would be least likely to care that he didn't know something. He suddenly pictured himself asking her. *Hey, Ali, do we still have duck doughnuts?* He could already see her face creasing in laughter even over such a ridiculous notion of a duck doughnut. *Bet this one was Abbie, getting the customers involved as well. Not today satan!*

Josh turned back to the two ladies chuckling.

"Almost had me there!" he smiled and walked away far too pleased with himself leaving the two of them confused.

9:07pm.

"Like what are we doing here?" Ali shrugged and Jackson raised their eyebrows. Ali stood at the end of the bar closest to the waitress station, fifth camomile tea clutched in her hands. The warmth of the cup on her palms felt more relaxing than drinking the tea itself. The slow clunking of the lift signalled the next table's food was being sent up. As the worrying mechanics behind the silver door finished and the light turned green Jackson pushed it open pulling out two large plates of fish.

"I know we are working, this is my job but what is the point? Am I contributing anything to society? I'm not helping stop global warming, I'm not fighting for human rights, I'm not saving lives..." Ali continued to talk while Jackson looked about the busy restaurant. Mingling conversation and laughter was echoing around the room. "You're right, I am making people happy." Jackson was still holding two dishes of monkfish hoping Ali would take them over to table six.

"Life is so tough and miserable. Maybe bringing joy and helping people relax is a worthy calling. Maybe that's all I need to do, because isn't the point of life to enjoy it?" Jackson offered her a smile and held out the fish again.

"Thanks Jacks." Ali smiled and finally reached to take the ridiculously large plates.

"I got it!" Abbie sped past stealing the plates from their position of passing over to Ali. The two of them shared a shrug as Danny sprinted past in the other direction, cork already half out the bottle he was opening.

9:48pm.

"Excuse me sir!" Josh called after a man who had slid off the stool by the top end of the bar and began to head for the door.

Josh trotted after the gentleman who looked to be in his early forties, wearing a pale linen shirt and brown trousers, he had been sipping a glass of wine slowly for a large portion of the evening, doing the crossword from the morning's paper, occasionally talking politely with Eddie.

Josh was pleased with his vigilance, catching the criminal as he tried to leave without paying.

"Sir!" Josh tried again.

"Josh." Eddie called after him. "He's fine josh."

Josh stopped in his tracks turning to Eddie.

"He runs the place next door." Eddie carried on, trying to explain. "Look, he found out he's got to close down a couple weeks ago, I've been giving him a few on the house since."

Josh stared. *Eddie wouldn't lie to you.* Eddie stared back. Josh continued staring. *He could be in on it.* Eddie didn't flinch or blink. Neither did Josh. *Trust no one.* Josh narrowed his eyes, holding his stare as he began to back away.

10:37pm.

The restaurant glowed. The lights turned down so dim customers needed to hold a candle to the dessert menu, but the intimate relaxed ambiance outweighed practicality. Abbie passed out desserts to the last large group in the restaurant, she had convinced the table of six which seemed to be on an awkward triple date that one of each was the best option. Whilst Danny swayed two men on a clearly very unimportant business meal that following a cheese board, port, sorbet and a bottle of dessert wine that whiskey was the best way to finish the night, suggesting a bottle which would need dusting off before pouring, it didn't take much convincing since the whole night was already written off on expenses. Molly had deemed herself incapable of human interaction and dedicated her full attention to polishing cutlery whilst Josh continued to misinform customers on the selection of Gins.

Josie bounded up the stairs, starting admin earlier tonight since service had gone so well.

"And that one goes well with Mediterranean tonic?" Josh asked Eddie again who nodded patiently, twisting the bottle of Gin impressively in his palm.
"Good service tonight boys." Josie interrupted whilst patting Josh on the shoulder. "How do you feel it went?" She asked Josh with a smile that was large even for Josie.
"Much better." Josh smiled back having managed to raise the bar from his trial shift which despite not being difficult he was still warranted some pride.
"Perfect!" She beamed before turning to Eddie. "I checked the kegs, and we didn't sell much of Waddle it be or Naked Ladies, I thought people might go for them even if just for the name." she shrugged. "Oh, and the Duck Doughnuts didn't shift much tonight so maybe you could create a good drink pairing to talk about at the briefing tomorrow to help push some sales." He nodded, whipping out a notepad to write down a reminder. "Could you put a reminder on there to remind me to order more Hoagie rolls as well. I know I'll forget otherwise."

Josh felt all the colour drain from his face as he looked down at his feet before shuffling away from the massive turd he had accidentally left for Josie.

Fuck. He kicked himself.

He glanced over his shoulder, feeling an uncomfortable adrenalin rush criminals must feel whilst weighing up whether or not to confess.

He took a step back toward Josie and Eddies conversation and clocked Jackson, staring at him through the gap between their heads. Jackson shook their head and held a finger to their lips. Josh gave a short nod of understanding before turning away.

Danny approached Abbie who was cashing off the final table at the till on the far side of the restaurant.

"Read it and weep!" he smugly leant against the large glass cupboard which behind held a ridiculous display of wine bottles in between old books with a layer of dust so thick you could draw in it.

Abbie turned to him from the till that processed the payment, it had a slight glitch whenever you closed a tab but for the past few months, they had all got used to ignoring.

"Oh yeah?" she asked as he fanned himself with the colourful assortment of notes in his hand.

"£160" he proclaimed proudly. "And 72 pence." he finished fishing out a couple of pennies from his jeans which were just dark enough to hide the dribble of sauce down the left leg.
"Wow." She looked almost impressed.
"Yep! Read it and weep!" he repeated proudly but he felt a small sinking feeling in his stomach. *Oh dear.*
"Oh dear." she sniffled and pretended to wipe her eyes. "Whatever shall I do?" she reached into her bra and pulled out a huge wad of notes. She dabbed at her eyes

with them before pulling out more from her back pocket and miming blowing her nose.

"£230" she grinned. "Oh and 80 pence." She pulled out coins from her pocket.

Danny stared at the money in silence. His face pouted in a disappointed defeat.

"Show off." he mumbled before grabbing the pennies in her hand and running off.

Not long after the Chefs began to emerge from their den downstairs. The youngest of the pack was a short boy, skinny in ripped jeans and a dark shirt, his long hair flopped over his eyes. He sat at the bar as a coke was placed in front of him and Josh watched wondering if he were actually old enough to drink. Matteo made his way up next.

On his way to his normal seat at the bar he poked his head round to the waitress station.

"Hey Al." he got her attention; and she looked over her shoulder but turned fully to face him when she registered it was Matt which meant he probably wasn't going to inflict another job on her. "Just wanted to check if you're ok?"
"Yeah, just having an internal philosophical breakdown."
"Oh yeah? How is uni going?" he asked with a cheeky grin. She laughed and turned back to the cutlery whilst he made his way further down the bar.

"Hey Matt, just wanted to say sorry earlier." Josh managed to catch him in transit before he reached his colleague, and the private apology became public.

"For what?" The chef looked confused for a brief moment before the distant memory of the beginning of service dawned on him. "Ah Don't worry about it. I blame Abbie."
"Why?"
"It's normally her fault somehow." He shrugged and took a seat where a beer was sitting waiting.

"How you feeling Al?" Abbie asked, interrupting the intense focus on polishing silverware.

"Yeah ok. Had a good talk with Jacks" Ali's words were positive, but her shoulders were low and her tone more deflated than normal after a Saturday night shift. "When did I get old? When did I go from wanting to change the world and chase my dreams, to being upset that my non-stick pan is no longer non-stick? Am I missing out on my own life by helping everyone else enjoy theirs?" She looked at Abbie as if hoping that her friend had the holy grail she had been hunting for in the bucket of cutlery.

"And miss hanging out with me and Danny every night." She grinned. "Look, one day we will be on the other side of it all. But until I make my millions, this aint bad." Ali smiled a real smile and Abbie gave her shoulder a squeeze. She reached into her back pocket and started flicking through her money.

"Here" she counted out half her tips and put them in Ali's hand.

"No, I can't." she protested holding them back out to Abbie and shaking her head and waving a hand casually.

"Half of them are yours anyway." Abbie winked and walked away.

Ali pushed the tips into her pinny looking about at the restaurant. Customers filtering out as the chefs slowly drifted to the bar, drinks already made waiting. Abbie and Danny spraying each other rather than the tables. Not long till the doors would be locked and there would be a Gin and tonic on the bar ready for her.

This wasn't so bad.

Welcome to the Bells

Volume 3

There was once a time Abbie gave a shit. That time was long past. Even looking in the review mirror all that was left of her last fuck was a bit of smoke on the horizon. She checked her watch. She was already late.

There was once a time she would be performing a hasty trot whilst frantically messaging Josie to apologise for being late. She wasn't sure she would run again... even if someone was chasing her.

Life is too short to take it too seriously. Life is too short to waste chances when they come along. And the chance that Danny, Ali and her all finished early were a million to one!

She grinned happily to herself looking forward to spending time with her best friends outside of the pub. Well, they might still go to a pub, but it would be a different one from where they worked. After that Abbie had in her bag a Tupperware full of fun they hadn't had since the summer solstice last year.

She strolled in calmly. The pub had a subtle buzz that befitted a Saturday lunch. Most of the walkways were taken up by buggies and highchairs, the few passages left open for the floor staff were littered with chips and peas that had been discarded by a child. The front windows were open in an attempt to let in a summer breeze but mainly let in faint wafts of cigarettes from groups of people who Abbie probably would have been smoking with if she didn't work every weekend.

She made her way casually to the end of the bar where Danny was pulling large plates full of fancy takes of classic pub grub. The burger stacked so high it would be an achievement to even take a bite, sandwiches filled with ingredients they all pronounced differently and fish that was probably still swimming the same morning.

"Morning!" she nodded to Danny.
"Afternoon!" he nodded back.
"Bloody sunny innit?" Abbie blew out her breath.
"Ah shall I compare thee to a summer's day?" Danny laughed whilst comically looking deeply into the reflection of himself in her large sunglasses.
"Always welcome at a Barbeque?" She smiled whilst pushing her glasses onto her head.

"What time do you call this?" Josie asked, interrupting the laughter whilst tapping her watch as she made her way over to them both. Her usual bright smile was hiding frustration.
"Early." Abbie answered without missing a beat.
"Abbie starts at five today, Josie?" Danny chimed in with a quizzical expression. Josie looked back and forth between them. If she were a machine, IT would be advising

turning her off and on at this point.

"Sorry I thought I put you down for a four thirty start, but I must be wrong." She waved her hand as if wafting away her mistake and wandered off herself.

"Thanks for covering." Abbie smiled.

"Anytime." He grinned back. "More importantly. How is tonight looking?"

"Tonight is looking tasty if I do say so myself." She pulled out a medium sized Tupperware and placed it in front of him. "Ma's recipe with a little twist."

"You didn't make them as strong as last time, did you?" he looked down at her with a small grimace as the memories of last time surfaced.

"No no." Abbie laughed as she also remembered. "Last time was maybe a bit much, best sleep I've had since the womb though."

Danny picked up the box and held it close to him.

"Still can't believe the three of us are all finishing at ten!" he grinned.

"Touch wood." They both chimed in sync whilst tapping the bar quickly.

Scott emerged at the top of the stairs and Danny quickly pushed the box onto the side of the waiter's station.

"Just coming up to let you know." Scott started and glanced down to his notepad.

"Excuse me." Josh slid past unnoticed. Danny and Abbie kept their eyes and broad smiles directed at Scott.

"Just to let you know, we only have two portions of the hake left and have run out of the burgers now." He turned away before they could respond.

"Yes Chef." Danny called after him and he stopped in his tracks, halting so fast the top half of his body jerked as it struggled to stay in sync with the bottom half. Scott turned slowly and stalked back to Danny. Looking down his large nose at both of them.

"What was that?" he asked sharply, his gaze bearing deep into Danny's before turning the same glare on Abbie who quickly pushed her glasses back down.
"Erm... Acknowledgement of what you said." Danny innocently proclaimed whilst looking to Abbie who joined him in surrender.

"No, that was respect..." his finger pointing accusingly. "You two fuckers are up to something... and when I figure out what it is you'll be on Sunday doubles for a month." The two of them began a silent protest of gasps and shrugs. "I've got my eye on you both!" he lingered just long enough before storming off back to the kitchen.

Abbie slowly pushed her glasses back onto her head. "How does he always know?" She pondered. "He's got a good radar, that man, I would respect it more if he was less of a dick."
"Agreed." Danny shrugged and they turned around back to the box.

Both of them had forgotten Josh was behind them. He had finished punching through an order on the till which sat to the side of the coffee machine and had clearly decided he deserved a break as he sipped his coffee along with a large chunk of cake.

"Josh…" Abbie spoke slowly as if trying not to spook him.

"I'm sorry, are these yours? I thought you said food left here was ok to eat. I didn't have time for breakfast, and I don't know when my break is and-

"No no it's ok…" she spoke gently.

Shit. But we touched wood…

"Ali. Ali. Ali" Abbie ran over to Ali who was standing at the far waitress station gathering cutlery to finish setting up the restaurant. She turned round upon hearing the urgent call of her name. "Fuckin' 'ell Al." Abbie jumped back as she saw her friend. Ali's face was red and blotchy, covered poorly with a heavy layer of foundation which didn't match her skin tone, succeeding to add another colour to the artist's already incorrect palette.

"Is it really that bad?" She whined whilst turning to the till, trying to study her reflection on the till screen.

"No. no no…" Abbie tried to reassure her but the deep grimace on her face was as convincing as Prince Andrew's TV appearance. "Did you use that cheap moisturiser again?"

"No… I am trying to find my purpose in life." Ali started. "And top of my goals is to save the planet."

"Naturally." Abbie nodded along wondering which part of the planet punched her in the face.

"So I thought in the meantime before maybe getting a law degree and becoming an environmental lawyer or maybe getting an engineering degree and working out more ways to create sustainable energy." She carried on slowly edging toward an explanation. "I thought I'd be a bee-keeper." She finished pulling back a clump of hair in front of her eyes to show a horribly swollen eyelid. Abbie put a gentle hand on her shoulder.

"A worthy calling for sure. but perhaps not yours." She spoke and suppressed laughter.
"I'm not fully ready to laugh yet so can we carry this on after service." Ali looked away self-consciously.

"You still look beautiful, Al." Abbie smiled whilst lacing her arm behind her friends' shoulders and giving her a light squeeze. They stood together for a while, watching the steady flow of customers. Lunch groups swayed away after too much *rosé*, large buggies which had been filling every possible route around the restaurant were finally removed as the families left to stroll in the sun on the common opposite.

They watched as Josh fumbled around awkwardly carrying the ridiculous Picasso inspired variety of dessert plates. He was clumsy and slow.

"Oh." Abbie casually pulled away from the hug. "Josh accidentally ate one of tonight's brownies." Ali's eyes flew as wide open as the bee stings would allow.

6:00pm

"OK Team" Scott started the evening briefing. He slapped a freshly printed stack of menus onto the end of the bar, narrowly avoiding a splodge of ketchup. The entire front of house team had gathered before him, minus

Josie who continued to ignore briefing and instead swept up the explosion of fries from an earlier toddler.

"Nothing much has changed… Jesus Ali have you been using that shit moisturiser again?" Ali let out a deep sigh.

"Just a few bee stings." she shrugged it off as if it wasn't making every blink painful.

"Right…" Scott continued. As I told Danny earlier, no more burgers and only two hakes. I doubt he passed it onto the rest of you." Scott raised his eyebrows at Danny who didn't hear the insult but stared instead at Josh. Scott followed his gaze and Josh became visibly uncomfortable, giving a small smile he looked down fully invested in the minuscule changes to the menu.

"This afternoon was a bit messy." Scott continued. "There were modifications that made no sense and way too many of them. I don't want to have to keep coming up here during service so if tables are being difficult just ask Abbie for a hand." He nodded at Abbie who also wasn't listening but staring deeply at Josh. Scott looked back to Josh again who looked behind him but saw only a sparse restaurant.

"Let's have a good service everyone!" Scott finished giving Josh another look in an attempt to understand why he had suddenly become so interesting. Most of the team dispersed leaving behind only Danny, Abbie and Josh.

"Do I have something on my face?" Josh asked, rubbing the side of his mouth and cheeks.

"No no no." Abbie began to protest. "Nothing there!" She gave him a huge smile and he strolled away feeling uncertain, glancing back at them both.

"You look fantastic mate!" Danny called after him.

"Bit far." Abbie snorted.

"What are we going to do?" Danny asked "It's gunna kick in soon..." he pondered whilst watching Josh fumble his way round the restaurant. He was evidently attempting to relay tables, carrying around forks and knives. Holding out his hands in L shapes to constantly check which was left and right, then doubling back realising knives go right not left.

"Sure, it hasn't kicked in already?" Abbie giggled as they watched him shuffle along, Ali hot on his heels fixing every mistake.

"We need a plan..." Danny said, clicking his tongue to indicate he was at least attempting to think.

"We could send him home sick?" Abbie pushed the first idea on the table but they both began to laugh at the thought of a hospitality worker being sent home early even if projectile vomiting.

"I think we are going to have to somehow do the shift with him without anyone noticing." Danny stated the obvious and impossible.

"Ok, you watch him and keep him out of trouble, and I'll do his section and mine." She proposed.

"Easy." Danny said, slightly unsure.

"What could go wrong?"

"It's all wrong." Danny exclaimed, holding out the tickets to Abbie who bit her lip.

They looked down at the tickets in Danny's hands whilst Eddie stood confused over their shoulder.

"They must be going somewhere." He gestured to the mass of perfect drinks he had made for what turned out to be non-existent people at non-existent tables.

"We will figure it out." Abbie reassured him. Eddie walked away with a grumpy shrug.

"He's not doing good." Danny stated the obvious as Josh stood still, two empty glasses in his hands. His face tilted toward the air con. "Suppose not as bad as Al's trial shift."

"Right, I'll get rid of the drinks. I'll just take them to random tables pretending they are the right order and just hope some of them are." She took her idea and ran before she could find a flaw in it.

Abbie had succeeded in giving away two thirds of the drinks whilst Danny watched as Josh stayed content underneath the air con. As she loaded up another tray she turned around quickly to immediately bump into.

"Harry?" Abbie exclaimed in shock as a very tall boy around her age was suddenly in her way. His head was shaved but he kept a trimmed beard, his loose jeans looked like they would drop off his skinny legs any moment and his shirt looked to be the same he wore on their only date a year ago... didn't look like it had been washed since either.

"How are you?" he smiled. She let out a huge sigh, already bored at the déjà vu happening in front of her.

"Really busy." she nodded at the full tray of drinks in her arms.

"You always said that?" he scoffed and rolled his eyes. Abbie was trying to weigh up if he was joking or not.

"Because it's the truth." she laughed back in his face whilst trying to shuffle around him.

"When can I see you next?" He stepped into her path again.

"How about the 31st of June?" she offered sarcastically once again trying to shuffle around him.

"Come on Abbie." he pleaded, moving a step closer. She moved the tray of drinks from its balanced position on her right hand in front of her as an alcoholic barrier. "You never gave us a chance."

"Harry, I don't know why you are acting like we had more than one date." she spoke fast and harshly, getting bored.

"Exactly. Only one date. Give me another chance." he smiled trying to move closer.

"Peter Parker gave Green Goblin a second chance. Look how that turned out." She called over her shoulder as she pushed past him and began dropping drinks off to people's tables. When she reached the comfy table in the corner, she saw the empty wine glass and approached the gentleman sitting alone in an ugly jumper.

"Can I get you another?" she asked, nodding at the empty glass.

The man didn't look up or answer but kept his nose buried deep into the pages of his book.

"Sir?" she nudged him.

"Oh god, I'm so sorry!" he suddenly jumped.

"What are you reading?" Abbie asked, twisting her head to peer at the cover. He lifted it up to show her. It was a dull grey cover with a silhouette on it. could have been about anything.

"It's about the assassination of a politician which led to the rise of the Nazi party."

"Spoiler alert, they win the election." Abbie joked picking up his glass. "Another?"

"Please!" he smiled watching as she walked away before turning back to his page.

Abbie approached the till at the end of the restaurant. Ali was pushing through a ridiculously long order, Abbie watched impressed as she didn't even glance at her notepad, even when beginning to push on the main courses.

"Who was that?" Ali asked, raising her eyebrows but not turning away from the till as she modified 'chips not mash' on another fish dish. Abbie winced in the knowledge that Scott will storm up with the ticket. She hastily added 'they are children sorry!' even though they both knew that would do nothing to aid the wounded artist.

"The guy with the book? no idea." Abbie shrugged off her question.

"The one by the bar." Ali turned to her as she sent the order.

"You remember that one night stand last year?"

"The one that wanted to watch Harry Potter whilst you guys-

"Yep, that's him" Abbie nodded back over to Harry who was also looking at them. Ali raised her hand and gave him a wave.

"He definitely looks your type." she laughed.

"I don't have a type." Abbie snorted and flicked a stray hair that had fallen from her precariously constructed ponytail. "What's my type?" asked suddenly concerned.

"Wrong for you." Ali giggled and Abbie lightly thumped the top of her arm.

"At least it's not dead German overthinkers." Abbie laughed. Now it was Ali's turn to hit back.

"We are not a day care!" Scott appeared behind them furiously with the ticket crumpling between his grasps. He didn't wait for a response before turning back to storm down the stairs.

"You want me to kick out a five-year-old?" Ali called after him, throwing her hands up in surrender.

"I'll do it if you need?" Abbie shrugged and Ali whacked her round the head with her order pad.

7:23pm

"Look." Abbie started calmly as they stood next to the dispense. Luckily it was still relatively early in the service, few tickets sat on the rail and Ali was easily spreading her attention between all the tables. "Josh." she continued slowly putting a gentle hand on his shoulder.

"We." she carried on gesturing to herself and Danny. Josh looked back and forward between them. Sweat dripped from his forehead. "Do you remember that little snack you had earlier?" Josh's face showed no sign of clarity. "That perfect cooked, delicious, moist, chocolate brownie? probably melted in your mouth? Maybe the best thing you ever tasted?" Abbie continued to try and jog his memory. "Well...

"Josh you're high." Danny cut in as the lift let out a high ping, signalling its arrival. Abbie gave him a slow glare of disapproval.

Panic filled Josh's face. He flushed a deep red, regretting the white shirt which highlighted the increase in his sweating.

"You wanted an ice bucket?" Eddie plonked one down in front of them. Abbie gently took Josh's hands and slowly submerged them in the bucket of cold water.

"Everything is going to be fine." She continued with her soothing tone.

"Is it?" Danny muttered underneath his breath, and he gave him another slow glare.

"We are here for you." Abbie smiled.
"Look mate." Danny interjected. "If you need to go home, we can-
"No, I can't go home." the rush of words spilled from his mouth. "My mum..."
"It's ok, it's ok." Abbie calmed him. "We are going to look after you." Josh smiled feeling reassured. However, he didn't know Abbie well enough yet to know she couldn't look after a basil plant longer than one Bolognese.

"Anyway." Danny slapped on a large uneasy smile. "Just think of it as practice for uni eh?"

Abbie rolled her eyes so hard they were close to tumbling out their sockets.

7:58pm

"I just needed to double check." Matteo spoke whilst holding out a ticket to Danny. "Are you sure this is right?"

Danny looked down at the ticket. Immediately seeing Josh's name on the top, he knew the answer was no.

"I'll just ask Josh." Matteo spoke fast with agitation whilst running his hand through his curly black hair.

"No no no." Danny grabbed his wrist firmly, stopping him from leaving.
"Six portions of chips does seem a bit too much for a table of two." Danny wanted to revel in the moment of back of house staff using common sense but knew now wasn't the time.
"It's wrong." Danny answered decisively. "I'll void it, and sort it out." he finished, still grasping his arm tightly. The chef pulled his arm sharply from Danny's grasp and left to go back downstairs, glancing back at Danny who still had a nervous smile plastered across his face as he scanned the room for Josh.

Failing to spot Josh he saw Ali instead and decided she was the best bet.

"Any more drinks or sauces." She asked after popping the final plate down.

"Salt and pepper?" one lady asked.

"It's in the middle of the table."

"I'm missing a fork." the younger gentleman started looking up at her expectantly as if she could pull the utensil out her arse.

"It's under the side of your plate sir." She pointed out kindly, abruptly ceasing the search.

"Are you sure this is gluten free?" The first lady asked again.

"Yes, it is." Ali smiled and turned away before anyone else could open their mouth. "Fuckin ell." she cursed as she turned to find Danny towering over her an inch away. "Announce yourself next time." she said, wide eyed shaking off the initial shock.

"Where is Josh?" He demanded quickly.

"Excuse me, could I have some Dijon mustard." The lady behind Ali called to her loudly, pronouncing Dijon in a way that would launch her fully into a story of how she spent a six-month sabbatical in the Dordogne.

"Of course." Ali called over her shoulder, her pitch raising back up a few decibels to add to the facade that she cared for their condiment selection. "I don't know where he is." She admitted with a shrug. "Why?"

Danny flipped the ticket toward her with wild panic in his eyes. "He's got the munchies."

8:12pm

"Can't believe it." Ali laughed as Abbie rhythmically but gently hit her head against the wall. The two of them stood by the coffee machine, hidden from view behind the wobbly wooden panelling. Ali sipped on her fourth green tea, holding a napkin full of ice to her swollen face.

"Hey Al, I've just put a new table…is everything ok?" Josie interrupted herself upon seeing Abbie who had now slumped down onto her knees. Face still firmly pushed into the wood.
"James is here…" Ali explained.

"I can get rid of him if you want Abbie." Josie quickly offered and Abbie pulled herself back onto her feet.

"Thanks Jose but it's ok… it's been like seven years." Abbie tried shrugging it off.

"You know it takes between seven to ten years for all the cells in your body to be replaced so you are pretty much a completely different person now." Ali tried to help.

"I just wish he had gotten fat or shaved his beard." Abbie blew out her breath as they peered around the corner of the waitress station at table six where James sat. His natural tan glowing behind a perfectly trimmed beard, white teeth gleaming through his laughter, deep green eyes sparkling from even this distance. He leant over to take the hand of the girl he was with, she was too tall for him, legs so long they were a trip hazard. Long blond hair shone as it moved, even the ambient lighting of the restaurant seemed to ripple off of it with every swish it should come with its own photosensitivity warning.

"Well…" Josie spoke breaking the trance the couple had them in. "There are always plenty more fish in the sea." She pushed a large smile on her face and gave Abbie a light squeeze on her shoulder before leaving the two of them.

"You know what else is in the sea." Ali looked at Abbie and sipped her tea. "Trash."

Abbie looked back over to her first love. A long-lost feeling swelled in her, looking at the girl that used to be her. Danny ambled past them one hand on Josh's shoulders, steering him through the restaurant apologising, the other hand holding a small brown plate which served bread and butter. The normally perfect scoop of butter had been punctured with a clumsy finger. A smile of childlike glee was spread across Josh's face as he swallowed stolen bread.

8:27pm

"Come on Eddie. I need your help."
"I don't want any part of it." He shook his head, keeping his eyes on garnishing the two highball glasses of gin. The sprigs of rosemary poked out the top of them were filling Abbie's nostrils, she pondered why anyone wanted a drink that smelt like a bath bomb but wasn't going to insult her opposition during an important business transaction.

"Come on, we can come to an arrangement." Abbie pushed him. Jackson and Eddie exchanged glances.

"What would be your terms?" Eddie asked.

"Jackson comes on the floor tonight."

"Nope." He shut her up, shaking his head. "You've opened this can of worms, now you must lie in it." Jackson smiled at him but put a hand on his shoulder and cocked one eyebrow. "Only if you are sure, Zenoria."

"And your terms?" Abbie asked eager to finish the deal as she saw Josh turning the milk steamer off and on in her peripherals.

"We want one." He spoke with no room for negotiation.

Jackson raised their eyebrows. "Each?" Abbie asked in shock.

"Fine…" she muttered and they both grinned. Jackson didn't waste time pulling Josh away from the coffee machine and plonking him in front of a half-polished tray of glasses, pushing a cloth in his hands before striding onto the floor with ease.

Abbie started another lap of the restaurant, by the time she had reached the man in the jumper again her brain was holding five drinks orders and her hands a full tray of wine glasses.

"Yes." he started before she could even ask. "Same again please."
"No problem at all." she smiled, adding another glass to the tray with ease.

"I am Simon by the way." he gave an awkward wave.
"Abbie." She introduced herself. "I'd shake your hand

but mine are pretty full." She forced a laugh.

"Good to meet you." he smiled again. She stood by his table a moment longer before realising that was her social cue to leave.

Abbie turned around with a sigh of relief, as she deposited the tray onto the bar and her arm relaxed into a tense flop now the weight was off of it.

"Abigale?" a voice behind her asked. She took a deep breath and looked up to the sky wondering why her karma was so out of balance today.

"Hi Michael." She turned to face another bad memory in her love story.

"It's great to see you." He grinned, taking a step toward her. She took one back. "How have you been?" He asked, taking a step toward her whilst she took another back. "You never replied to my last text." He continued as their dance carried her right back to the other end of the bar. "Just thought we could maybe…"

"I'm not free." She laughed realising she needed to end the conversation before she ended up in table one's bowl of soup.

"Abbie, can you take this food out please." Danny called to her in a rush whilst slamming open the lift in a hurry and pulling down a ticket waving it in her face.

"Sorry Michael." she gave an awkward smile before moving over to Danny.

"Yeah sure, no problem, another time then." He stuttered out. "I'll see you around." he finished whilst slowly backing up still watching her. He only turned away when he was halfway out the door. Josie watched him leave with a quizzical expression before noticing he was talking to

Abbie and shrugged it off as another odd acquaintance, she had somehow managed to make.

"Thanks Danny." she breathed a sigh as he closed the lift and put the ticket back in place.

"Who was that?" He laughed watching as Michael continued to stand just outside of the door watching them both. Danny gave him a wave and he blushed so deeply he looked ill.

"Michael." she let her head fall into her hands and groaned loudly.

"Is he the one who took you to build a bear for your second date?"

"No, he invited me to his dog's birthday to meet his parents." She started the sentence frustrated but couldn't help but join Danny in laughter by the end.

"As Auden says, if equal affection cannot be, let the more loving one be me."
"I'm good, thanks."

"That reminds me though." Danny said, pulling out a notepad from his pocket and scribbling illegible words. "Becca wants to come in next Sunday with her parents."
Great timing. Abbie thought with a deep sigh.

"Sorry. Not a good time to mention my functional relationship." He apologised with a smirk, pushing the notepad back into the pocket of his tight jeans whilst she thumped the top of his arm.
"It's fine. I'm happy that you don't have to swim around the dating pool."
"Is it really that bad?" Danny laughed.

Abbie shrugged but if this were a real pool, the water would be cold, the wave machine broken and stuck on full blast and a kid would be pissing in the corner.

8:47pm

Eddie watched Josh closely whilst twisting the rim of two margarita glasses in salt.

"What happened next?" Josh asked, leaning halfway over the bar, completely wrapped up in the story. Across from him, sipping a Brandy Alexander was Alec, one of Eddie's favourite customers who popped in a couple of times a week, normally in a vintage three-piece suit, he took Eddie's recommendations and when he didn't his own choices were impeccable. A true man of class, with a million stories… which were all clearly ridiculous lies told by a confused old man, but he broke up Eddie's week, and his works of fiction were at least very entertaining.

Alec currently had Josh engrossed with the tale of his time in America in the 1970s.

Eddie smiled to himself, at least Josh was out of trouble. He scanned the crowd, watching as Jackson had effortlessly stacked up a table of eight plates and Abbie looked like she was doing a magic trick with how her glasses were balanced.

"So, son." Alec started after another sip of his drink. "Word of advice, if you aren't sure, don't eat it."

Eddie almost laughed. *Bit late for that.*

9:18pm

"What did you do?" Danny ordered an answer from him whilst pointing at Josh who sat on the floor behind the bar. His back pressed against the fridge, hands clasping a coffee mug filled with a small amount of foamy liquid. He let out small rhythmic sobs.

"Well thought some alcohol might chill him out and some coffee would get him more alert so boom. Espresso martinis!"

"Everything feels wrong." he cried. "I don't want to be here."

"Yeah none of us do, buddy." Danny took the mug of martini off him and pulled him to his feet. He put his arms round him and Josh clung back, Danny was slightly taken aback as Josh was stronger than he looked. "It'll pass mate. Just got to wait it out."

"Wow." Josh pulled away looking at Danny as if he just revealed the secret to immortality or figured out who jack the ripper was. "That's so true. Life is just waiting it out in different ways."

"As Fall Out Boy wisely said, if death is the last appointment, then we're all just sitting in the waiting room" Danny is always happy when Fall Out Boy could naturally slide into conversation. Josh's face crumbled from its philosophical break through into tears again.

"Bit much." Eddie whispered before turning away, elegantly tossing a napkin onto his shoulder as Josh buried his face further into Danny's retro patterned shirt. He looked around the restaurant trying to catch the eye of Abbie or Ali.

Abbie was power walking around the restaurant, piling glasses onto her tray with the confidence of someone who has never lost a game of Jenga.

"One more maybe?" She asked Simon, the lone gentleman with his book as his wine glass was once again empty.
"Oh you're a bad influence." Simon laughed, temporarily putting his book down.

"I knew that already." she replied, forcing a small chuckle.

"I think I'm ready to change it up a bit. Do you have any pink gin?"
"Oh well it's not pink but we have a lovely raspberry gin. All the same flavours as Pink gin minus the diabetes." She smiled as he burst out laughing, it was the third time she had used that joke in this service alone, but this was the best reaction to it.

"I'm sold." he continued to laugh as she turned away, clocking Josh clinging to Danny like he was the last plane out of Saigon.

"Abbie." Josie intercepted her as she approached the bar. "I'm sorry but your friend with the shaved-

"He's not my friend." Abbie interrupted not looking at Josie but over her shoulder to Josh and Danny. Danny had managed to get free enough to turn round so he could scrape down the empty plates and load them up ready to be sent back down whilst Josh was still latched onto him from behind.

"Oh ok. Well, he's definitely had one too many so I was going to see if you could politely ask him to leave, but I'll ask Danny..." she trailed off letting out a large sigh and running her hand through her hair.
"No no no." Abbie quickly coaxed her back, whilst depositing the tray of empty glasses on the side of the bar. "I can sort it."
"Ok thank you." Josie smiled wearily. "What a strange shift eh?" she let out a small laugh.
"You know Jose." Abbie began, already regretting taking out the gun and pointing it at her foot. "You have been working so hard. you should go home and I'll lock up tonight with Danny." Abbie finished, pulling the trigger.
"Are you sure? Josie's whole body deflated in relief. "Thank you, Abs."

"Yeah, you should go home. you've been working really hard." Abbie continued looking physically in pain as if she really had put a bullet in her foot.

"Thank you, Abbie." Josie smiled and pulled her in for a hug. Abbie was taken aback at first, but she settled into the unexpected embrace, not realising how much she needed it. "By the way I know Josh is high as a kite and I'm sure you are involved somehow." she whispered in her ear and pulled away. Abbie tried to smile through the grimace. Josie pulled the keys for the pub out her back pocket and plonked them rattling into Abbies hands. "Don't burn the place down." she almost skipped off, leaving Abbie pulling in a deep breath.

She turned round to survey the situation catching Danny's eye as Josh continued to spoon him. She held up the keys letting them jangle. Danny Let his head flop forward in defeat.

10:20pm

"Well, that's the last dessert out." Abbie sighed whilst assessing the restaurant. Ali was doing her best to clean down tables. Jackson had returned to the bar to try and push through the swollen mass of glasses that Eddie had been too busy to sort through during service. The dirty plates were piled so high and balanced so delicately that if they were anywhere else it could have been an art exhibit under the name 'a view from the bottom of the ladder'.

Ali approached Abbie and Danny at the dispense area. "How's cutlery coming? I can't lay anymore till we have more polished." The three of them turned to Josh who had been hidden in the wooden crevice of the waitress station still polishing the same knife he had been for just under an hour.

"Well one knife is perfect." Danny attempted the glass half full approach, even if right now he needed a glass very full of vodka.

"Come on then." Ali ushered Josh over to her. He followed with no objections as she helped hoist him up onto one of the bar stools. Eddie had a glass of water sitting ready for him.

As the first of the Chefs began to climb their way up the staircase into the darkness of a bistro pub trying too hard to be ambient.

Matteo made his way straight over to them. Abbie decided going in hard with small talk might distract from the mess of the evening and the mess which still surrounded them.

"Hey, Mattie how was your…"

"Which one of you guys got Josh high?" Matteo cut her short laughing to himself.

"It was Abbie." Danny's words rushed out his mouth faster than Usain Bolt. Abbie looked over to him in disgust, whilst Matt walked off laughing. "What?" Danny looked shocked.
"Excuse me whilst I call the pest control." Abbie started. "Because I can see a rat." she tutted before turning away.

"Come on Ab's." he pleaded, turning her round to face him. "I promise next fuck up is on me."
"Nearly every fuck up is on you Danny." she tutted.

"Wow." he pulled away, offended with a hand on his heart to ease the pain of what they both knew was the truth. "So casually cruel in the name of being honest."
"Who said that?"

"Taylor Swift."

Matt approached the pint already waiting for him next to Josh's water.

"Alright Al?" he asked, propping himself up on the chair. She looked up to him with a smile having finished helping Josh balance on the stool. "Woah." concern creased across his face as he saw hers for the first time that night. In the chaos she had almost forgotten the swollen lumps even more poorly covered than when she had clocked in as most of her make-up had melted off in the sweaty business of covering two people's jobs whilst aiding in babysitting.

"No, I'm not using the cheap moisturiser again." She sighed looking away.

"Looks like you've had a fight with a beehive." he smiled.

"You're Not far off."

"Ah well you still look great." he took a long sip of his pint. "I'll watch him for you." he gestured to Josh.

"Thanks Matt."

11:42pm

With Josh under the care of Matt, the three of them had sped through all their jobs as quickly as they would have when they first started at the Bell's and wanted to make a good impression.

"What's the plan?" Ali asked, looking at Danny who quickly looked at Abbie.

"You take Josh home." Abbie pointed at Danny.
"I don't know where he lives..." he interrupted quickly.

"Ok Al take Josh home." Abbie began again glancing over to Josh who was sat up on a stool by the bar, the large glass of water lay untouched in front of him as he stared deeply into it as if it held all the answers to life's questions. "Ok both of you take Josh home, and I'll write the report, finish up and lock up."

"You sure?" Molly asked, scanning the whole room quickly. There were only three customers left, all with empty drinks, all very aware they were overstaying their welcome but making no move to leave either.

"Yeah, once Eddies finished on the bar, we just need to throw the bins out and we are done." she summed it up easily.
"Just don't put any puns in the report." Danny cautioned whilst he and Ali headed over to Josh.

12:02pm

Abbie felt a huge flood of relief as she twisted the key in the lock. At least it was over.

Even the worst days have to end.

She put Ali's bag and coat at her feet and lit a cigarette waiting for the others to come back.

"Hi." A male voice in the dark briefly made her jump before remembering she took karate lessons as a child. The man took a step forward and Abbie wasn't pleased to have to look at his hideous jumper again.

"Sorry we are closed." She gestured to the dark, locked building behind her.
"My place isn't." he chuckled. "Just wondering if you want to come back for a drink."
"Thanks but I'm ok. I'm just waiting for my friends."

"Could have come up with a better excuse." he laughed again but this time with a small hint of frustration. "Come on one drink." he tried again.

"No thank you." Abbie refused again whilst looking down the street praying Ali and Danny would appear around the corner.

"Come on, we had something in there." He pushed again, taking a step closer, coming further into the dim glow of the streetlamp.

"What you had in there was good service!" Abbie tried to control her temper, but fear was creeping up on her.

"One drink." he said again, getting even closer.

"Fuck off." Abbie tried to exert authority, but it came out fragile and empty. She wanted to move further away but all that was behind her was the door she had just locked.

"Give me a chance."

"Hey." Danny called from behind him, his voice was rough and deep, different from the voice that recited poetry all day. "She said fuck off." He spat whilst squaring up to him. The man backed off slowly with hands raised in surrender.

"Sorry mate, didn't realise." he turned away only to bump straight into Ali. Her eyes blazing in fury.

"You don't owe him an apology." she snapped. "You own her one." the man mumbled a halfhearted apology over his shoulder before crossing the road away from them and disappearing into the darkness of the badly lit streets.

"You ok Abs?" Danny asked, taking a step closer.

"No." she spat. *Fuckin patriarchary.* She threw her cigarette on the floor and stamped it out.

Ali took a step forward, taking one of Abbie's hands in hers. "I know babe."

"Men." she rolled her eyes. There was little anger now, exhaustion and frustration, but anger on this subject had all run out over the years.

"I know babe." Ali repeated, pulling her into a hug.

Danny put his arms around both of them, his tall body engulfing them, like a tree growing around two rocks. "I don't have many words of my own, but I could offer you some of Maya Angelou's?"

"Right." Abbie pulled away and pulled her smile back up. "Let's go have a brownie and watch Moulin Rouge."
"Aren't we all on the morning shift tomorrow?" Ali knew the answer but felt the need to inject at least some reason into the night.
"Yes… but Josie isn't?" Danny gave a cheeky smile and a small shrug.

Ali put her arm around Abbies shoulder as they began to walk in the direction of her house. Danny slid his hand into hers and gave it a squeeze.

Welcome to the Bells

Volume 4

No one ever grows up saying they want to work in hospitality. When asked as a child what you want to do you might say vet, weatherman, astronaut, superhero.

Josie had a to do list on an order pad it was smudged and sweaty and from being in her back pocket most the week and she wished it was illegible. Unfortunately, she could read it. timesheets, pays lips, fruit order, spirit order, wine order, kitchen invoice, cleaners' invoice, rota, holiday requests, wastage, breakages.

When you get asked as a teenager what you are trying to pursue, maybe you would say law, medicine or trying to make it in a band.

She rubbed her temples as she remembered the new wines. Add it to the menu, put it on the till, attempt to educate the staff about it... only after she had educated herself.

When you finish education, what do you hope for? A job that pays rent and some, a role where you are passionate, committed, or maybe just to accidentally become

YouTube famous and live off the millions made from people watching you yodel in a supermarket.

Who would want to work every weekend? Who wants to be paid the minimum possible? Who would want their sole purpose to ensure everyone has the best night possible whilst telling their own friends and family they can't make another birthday?

Life is all about balance. Engineering, Algebra, how often you see your extended family. It's all a balance. So why didn't she have any.

So, when asked why you work in hospitality, what do you say?

Josie wasn't sure anymore. She sat staring at the computer screen in the tiny office watching the emails ping in. Muffled music from the kitchen was floating under the shut door. From the playlist it sounded like someone was having a breakdown in 2006 – definitely Carlin, the youngest chef's turn to pick the music.

She took a breath and clicked on the first email.

The phone rang.

"Good morning, The Bells, Josie speaking, how can I help?" she answered like an automated message.

"Afternoon! I am just trying to book online for dinner tonight and it doesn't seem to let me." The cheery voice on the other end spoke. He sounded like a nice man, probably in his 50's, probably drinks real ale, probably won't be happy with their selection.

"Oh dear, I am sorry, let me open our booking system and check what is going on." Josie left the office and climbed upstairs looking for the iPad with the bookings on. After faffing with it for a while she apologised to the man, took his details and promised a table and hung up.

The app opened and closed abruptly, it logged in and froze, it crashed and died every attempt. *Bloody technology.* She mentally cursed Steve Jobs. She wasn't sure why but lots of things seemed to be his fault so why not this as well.

"Jose." Scott called from the top of the stairs.
"What's happened?" she asked, her tone clipped, still frustrated with him but promising herself it wouldn't infringe on her professionalism.
"My meat delivery hasn't turned up. Have you had a call or email from them?"
"No." she answered but she was ignoring so many emails, maybe she had. "I will chase them up for you."

She felt it in her gut that today was not going to swing her way. But then again does any day?

4:00pm

Abbie walked in half asleep despite it being late afternoon. The restaurant was sparse, only a few people were left drinking after what must have been a quiet Saturday lunch. Something strange was in the air and it was more than just the smell of burnt herbs. She took another step further in the door and stopped to look down as her feet crunched on to something. Abbie stared at the floor confused, almost invisible she saw a line of small white granules. *Better clean that up before Danny gets too excited.*

Confused, she looked over to the bar where Eddie was prepping for the most popular cocktails, hoping he could shed some light, but all Eddie had to offer was a shrug and slightly raised eyebrows. She caught Ali's eye who was slowly relaying the few tables that had been in use during the day. Ali gave a wide-eyed shake of her head.

Suddenly Josie popped up from behind a table in the far corner.

"Abbie!" she smiled far too brightly for someone who got in at 8am.

"Jose…" Abbie nodded at her with caution in her voice. She walked over and he saw she had a pot of Maldon rock salt in her hand. "What are you doing?"
"Anything that springs to mind really!" she laughed. Abbie studied her. Her eyes were too wide, her smile too big, her body almost twitching.

She's finally cracked.

"Jose." Matteo called from the top of the stairs. "We found some more sage; did you want it?"

6:00pm

"What has happened Al?" Abbie probed her for an answer as they stood together by the dispense section of the bar waiting for Scott to come up to tell them exactly what he told them yesterday spiced up with some insults. Ali sipped slowly on her tea, enjoying the feel of the warm mug in her hands, whilst Abbie glared down at her triple espresso, trying to force it to cool faster through means of intimidation.

"I think it's just a sprain." She explained looking down at her ankle slightly bandaged. She had started training for a marathon to run raising money for the refugee crisis, she hadn't quite fallen at the first hurdle, but she had badly tripped only 2 kilometres into this morning's jog.

"I mean what happened to Josie." Abbie clarified.
"Oh I dunno, she was like this when I came in." They watched Josie through the window, she had crossed the road over to the park and was pacing up and down, eyes intent on the grass beneath her feet. "She asked me if I thought you had any horseshoes…"

"What? Why would I have any horse shoes?"
"I mean you do dress like a lumberjack." She looked Abbie up and down, from her dull yellow plaid shirt to her baggy jeans and dirt covered trainers.

"Lumberjacks don't ride horses." Abbie snorted.
"You would know."

"Good afternoon one and all!" Danny called from the doorway, his arms spread out, the sun bright enough to silhouette his long body. The only way to add more drama to the entrance would be if he had a smoke machine or confetti cannons.

"What the hell are you wearing?" Ali asked, shaking her head in disagreement.

"Oh this?" He casually gestured to the long silky silver shirt hung off his tall lanky frame. The buttons were tiny pearls which extended even down to the cuffs which were only millimetres too short for the runway.

Danny continued to approach them slowly, spinning and strutting before coming to a rest leaning on the bar as if it were a chaise lounge.
"Just a little something I had tucked away." He said, giving his quaffed blond hair a flick, which didn't stir from its intensely gelled sculpting.

"It's hideous." Ali shattered his fantasy at the exact time Abbie proclaimed, "It's fantastic."

"You know it's going to get ruined the first time someone asks for ketchup." Ali raised her eyebrows.
"Look." He started taking a deep breath. "I bought this shirt eight months ago. It's been perfectly ironed hanging in my cupboard since waiting for a Saturday night so it can fulfil its fabulous purpose. But every Saturday night I am here so alas the poor shirt has been left, waiting, watching as I pull out and put on less expensive shirts. but no more!" He slapped the side of the bar, so hard even

Eddie jumped from where he was emptying the beer drip trays at the other end. "Tonight. It will fulfil its destiny."

Abbie and Ali continued to stare.

"Well, I love it!" Abbie broke the silence. "It's so shiny, I could do my hair in it."
"You probably should do your hair." Danny politely suggested. Abbie reached up to feel if her plaits that she slept in had come out of place, deciding they hadn't she smoothed down some loose strands and thought no longer on the matter.
"I think you'll regret it." Ali spoke in a sing-song tone of a mother who thought she knew best.

"Just because you only wear black."

"It's smart, practical and doesn't show armpit stains." Ali casually defended her sensible position. "Plus makes laundry very easy." Danny getting flustered in the face of simple logic turned his fashion attack to Abbie.

"You own more plaid than a highland army." he diverted his offence.
"Don't know why you're coming for me. I'm in support."

"This was not the glorious reception this shirt deserved." his tantrum began to escalate.
"Do you want to walk out and do it again?" Abbie suggested.

"You two are just jealous." He whined. "It's Saturday night, you are dressed for a funeral, you are dressed for the battle of Culloden, and I am dressed for a party." He finished by firmly crossing his arms with a big huff.

"I'm surprised you know about the battle of Culloden." Ali spoke through another sip of tea.

"I am a man of great intellect." Danny scoffed. "And I've read Outlander."

"It's a lovely shirt." Abbie gently finished the conversation.
"Thank you." He said whilst gracefully flitting around them to the other side of the bar with elegance royalty could aspire to.

"Right team." Scott called to announce his presence as he barrelled up the stairs. "Long story short." he began the briefing. "We're fucked."

The front of house team all grimaced, except for Abbie who necked her coffee first.

"Our meat and fish delivery didn't turn up. We went to the butchers, but they had very little, so I have six specials for you and only four of each. Vegetarians are going to love us tonight because Veg is pretty much all we have." he spoke fast with frustration. "To try and ease the pressure off the lack of starters Thomas has come up with some extra desserts. As well as a Cheesecake and cinnamon doughnuts he had made an extra-large white chocolate crème brûlée which you can special. If you sell it to them at the beginning maybe, we can shift focus away from starters." No one dared interrupt at any point. "Here is the menu. I've crossed off what we don't have, put a count next to what we do, and the specials are on the back." he threw down the thick paper menu with more red marks and crosses then Abbies GCSE math's paper.

"I would print them off with changes, but we don't have any paper left so you'll just have to verbal it all tonight."

The four of them all looked at each other with fear in their eyes.

"Any questions?" Scott threw out his hands as an invitation to join the panic. "No? good!" He nodded at them all before turning to walk away.

"He didn't even insult anyone…" Abbie whispered to Ali.

He hadn't even reached the stairs before he spun back around.

"It is the hottest day of the year and the air con in the kitchen is broken. If anyone comes down with anything stupid, I have a water pistol and I will use it." he let his threatening glare rest on them all in turn before finishing. "And Danny, don't wear shirts brighter than your future."

Abbie patted Danny on the shoulder as everyone slowly dispersed. Danny looked down at the menus and clicked his tongue in nervous anticipation for the night. Eddie and Jackson were prepping the bar to his right, he could see the stock of lemons and limes massively depleted which led them to opt for an odd assortment of fruits Danny would only come across in a risky smoothie.

Now alone he looked down at his shirt and smiled, still confident in his choice. Danny pulled the cuffs down a little, straightened his collar, he caught his warped reflection in the silver of the food lift, letting a small smile creep onto his face.

"*And I'm feeeeeeeling good.*" Danny looked to the speaker in the corner of the restaurant where Michael Bublé read his mind. He let his smile widen as he strolled away from the dispense area just as the trumpets kicked in.

Danny approached Ali and Abbie as they looked deep in discussion at the far till.

"What's going on?" Danny asked as he approached, leaning his slender body against the glass cupboards.
"We think it's time." Abbie stated whilst Ali nodded assertively.

"Well, I'm glad you have decided to grow out your fringe Al but don't think it's that simple." Danny smiled and Abbie hit her palm against her forehead.

"We think it's time we give Josh his bottle." Abbie clarified.

"What's wrong with my fringe?" Ali asked, suddenly stressed as she combed it down with her fingers.

"But he still has a day left on the bet." Danny pointed out.
"It's time." Abbie settled the discussion not looking at either of them but at Josh who was pointlessly shuffling chairs by centimetres which would be knocked out of alignment the moment customers started filling in.

"Josh." Abbie called to him. He looked up, startled at the three of them staring in his direction. Abbie beckoned him over with a short nod of her head. He started making his way over with a smile, but it started to fall slowly. The three of them stood with straight backs, and silent.

"Why do I feel like I owe a mob money?" he looked at each of them in turn.

Danny let out a small laugh, patting Josh on the back as he left. Ali gave him a small smile before leaving him alone with Abbie whose expression had not changed.

"Walk with me Joshua." She ordered whilst strolling away not checking if he was following.

"There comes a time in every server's life." She started dramatically as they started a slow lap of the restaurant. "Where you really..." she trailed off, stooping down to pick up a stray butter knife off the floor whilst he waited in anticipation for the end of the sentence. "Lose hope." she finished.
"Oh." Josh's smile fell.
"You lose hope in the human race." she continued. "You realise that they are all really that stupid. That no matter how many times you top up their water for them they will still tip under 10% and most allergies are actually dietary preferences."

"I mean remember that woman last week with the allium allergy, you'd think she would come up with something more convincing." he laughed but Abbie's face remained unchanged as they finished their lap of the building ending back by the dispense section.

"That's actually a real one, it's like onions, chives and leeks." All the blood drained from Josh's face. "But what I'm saying is Josh." she carried on despite Josh's fear of manslaughter through mushroom risotto. "You are one of us."

Josh was confused as she ducked behind the waitress station, opening the cupboard by the coffee machine and pulling out an opaque green bottle which matched the collection of others by the coffee machine. It already had his name clumsily written down the side in sharpie. She passed the bottle over and he accepted it slowly, confused that it might get retracted. but once it was in his hands, fingers grasping around its cool metallic material, he knew this was no joke. *This is how it must feel to be knighted.*

"Thank you, Abbie." He held the bottle close to him, feeling a warm sense of pride and acceptance spread through his chest. Abbie had a soft smile on her face. He lowered the bottle and began to lunge in for a hug.

"What are you doing?" she held her hand up.

"Oh, I thought we were..." He stuttered. "Please don't take the bottle back."

"It's not just a bottle." she began to explain. "This is your ticket to the back bar." his eyes widened as he looked over to Eddie to the gleaming bottles of alcohol.

"I don't understand." Josh admitted, knowing that his stupidity now will save a lot more stupidity later on.

"When a wrong order is put through. or a drink sent back. or if Eddie makes a mistake."

"Nope." Eddie interrupted, not looking away from the four pints he was pouring simultaneously.

"When something goes wrong. It is put on the back bar." Abbie finished gesturing with a flourish to an empty space between the long array of bottles and empty water jugs. "It's ours for the taking." she nodded at the bottle. "Just don't get smashed on shift and you're all good." she patted him on the shoulder.

"Thank you." Josh spoke through a deep emotional breath. He placed his green bottle next to Abbie's red, Danny's blue and Molly's orange. Looking at them all with a broad grin before striding off into the restaurant.

"What are you up to?" Eddie asked whilst twisting a corkscrew deep into a bottle of rosé, his eyes narrowed resting on Abbie.

"Nothing." She smiled innocently.

"Hmmm." he pulled out the cork with a satisfying pop, his eyes still following her as she walked around the waitress station heading for her own bottle.

She sipped the cold lemonade inside, looking forward to the first incorrect order involving gin. Watching Josh fumble off collecting glasses. A dramatic orchestral overture started in her ears. She glanced up to the speaker confused as to why duel of fates was suddenly part of the Saturday night playlist.

6:30pm

"Danny." Ali came over the dispense holding out the iPad to him. "I need you to man the door, my section is getting busier."

"Where is Josie?" He looked around for her bright ginger hair.
"Still across the park."
"You and Abbie are going to have to do it together." he

gestured to the tickets already beginning to come through. "I'm going to be overrun soon putting together bar snacks, dealing with all these modifications. The KP hasn't shown up so Scotts asked me to rinse down plates which I don't know if I can do in this shirt."

"But you are the assistant manager, you have to be in charge when Josie isn't here." Ali tried again but he simply raised his eyebrows. A lump of blue fabric by the coffee machine caught Ali's eye. "What's that?"
"Spare t-shirt Becca dropped off in case." he explained. "Why am I the only one who thinks this shirt is a good idea? That THING!" He stressed pointing to the t-shirt. "Is actually something I sleep in; something would have to go very wrong for me to wear it out the house."

"Touch wood." They both chimed tapping the bar.

Ali tutted, turning to the door to see Josie stroll in.

She surveyed the scene around her as service was beginning to kick off. The drinking areas both inside and out were packed full of people who had spent the afternoon drinking across in the park, migrating over in search of more alcohol and more adequate toilet facilities. Most of the crowd was young, living off parents' credit cards whilst pretending they had difficult lives to escape from.

"Josie!" Ali exclaimed, relieved trying to pass the iPad to her. "I've only had to seat a couple so far, but the booking says more are coming in and two drinking tables have asked about availability in the restaurant."

Josie took the iPad off her and looked at the colourful bars filling the screen. She looked about again and let out a deep breath.

"You ok Jose?" Abbie asked as she passed her with a tray of empty glasses.

She looked at Abbie already exhausted. "Just couldn't find a four-leaf clover."

Abbie looked over to Danny who stood in position by dispense with his eyebrows raised, the ticket machine started chugging out the first order just as the Beatles came over the speakers asking for Help.

6:51pm

"Can you take away the potatoes and can I have some avocado instead?" The lady asked with a smile so entitled it probably went to private school.

"We don't have any avocados unfortunately." Josh replied politely if not confused. Her partner looked taken aback. He snorted before shaking his head looking back down at the menu. The lady screwed up her face in confusion and took off her thin glasses, placing them down before making deep eye contact with Josh. Perhaps believing if she connected enough with him, he might just pull one out his arse for her.

She scoffed slightly before proclaiming "It's the 21st century... what do you mean you don't have avocado?"

Josh smiled and began backing away slightly intimidated, promising to check anyway. He tried to locate Josie but settled for Ali who was passing him with an armful of empty glasses.

"Ali." He caught her attention.

"What's up?"

"I'm struggling with how to explain to a customer that we don't have avocados. They don't believe me for some reason."

Ali offered him a knowing smile of pain. "I understand." She knew better than others after a while working in a venue where steak doesn't automatically come with chips, that some customers believe behind the scenes anything is possible and the menu is just a guideline to what was on offer.

"Some people just think we are magicians." Ali reassured josh. "As much as I'd love to saw them in half, I don't fancy cleaning up after."

Josh appreciated the metaphor, but he was feeling anxious about returning to the table.

"I just don't know how to-

"I'll go speak to them." Ali smiled. Josh thanked her with a deep breath, heading to his new bottle on the back bar, needing a drink to relax, still feeling the woman's stare piercing into him.

Ali didn't need to ask which table it was, only a woman with a smile that miserable would want avocado instead of potato.

"Ali." Josie intercepted her.

"What's up?" She asked, happy to let the lady wait.

"Do you have any crystals?" She asked with a smile but there was an odd pleading in her eyes.

"No…why?"

"I just need some positive energy." Josie explained. "I thought since you are at one with the planet you might be able to help."

"If I was at one with the planet I would be on fire." Ali spoke plainly. She offered an apologetic shrug before departing to ruin someone's diet plans.

Josie looked around with a sigh, making a mental note to hire someone who knew witchcraft.

7:12pm

"Let me just check." Abbie said as sweetly as she could knowing full well already nothing positive would come from the kitchen. She turned away suddenly feeling lethargic at the problem ahead. Abbie hastily trotted down the stairs, picking up her strides as she made it into staff only territory.

"We got one!" Abbie shouted down to the kitchen as she pounded her way down the short corridor.

"Nope!" Scott shouted back as she turned the corner.

"We got a vegan!"

After several minutes of staring at the menu Scott and Jasmine, the sous chef, looked at each other shaking their heads. Jasmine took a deep breath, scratching her head.

Her long black braids were pulled back into a neat bun, her deep brown skin shone with perspiration, but she refused to unbutton her whites, determined to remain the image of professionalism despite the broken aircon. She had an air of still and calm that was out of place but welcome in the kitchen. Like a fish gently swimming whilst the red sea parted beneath her she remained unaffected by the chaos. She wiped her face with an already sodden towel and shrugged at Scott, with a small apology in her brown eyes.

"Anyone else?" Scott offered out to the busy kitchen. All the chefs took a deep breath.

Thomas, the pastry chef, looked up from the other end of the kitchen. He was tall and lanky, long blonde hair pulled back loose in a bun. His thin framed glasses steaming up so often he considered giving up and surrendering to a life of blur for the rest of the shift. He paused making his crème brûlée, regretting the decision of a special which involved a blow torch. "We could take the Seabass off the risotto, and –."

"Nope, cheese in it." Scott dismissed fast.

Carlin, the youngest of the team, looked up from portioning out his vegetables." What about some of that fresh pasta with -."

"Eggs in the pasta."

"How about a boiled carrot?" Christina, the sauce chef, laughed from where she was searing a lamb leg.

"Any other options?" Abbie asked knowing full well that time to customers was measured in a similar way to dogs. Every human year is around 7 to dogs. Every server's minute equates to 20 to customers. She could see the review in full caps on trip advisor already.

"Come on guys. Any other options?" Scott pushed his team.

"The door?" Matteo called.

7:32pm

"Excuse me." A man in his late thirties approached the bar.

"Yes, sir, how can I help?" Eddie smiled leaning a little over the bar to hear him better.

"I was just wondering if you take requests?" he smiled politely whilst adjusting his tie. The man was dressed like a gender reveal party from his light pink suit and baby blue tie. Eddie could see he was a man of unique taste; it might not be a taste anyone else enjoyed but taste nonetheless.

Eddie straightened his own navy bow tie, ready to flex his creative muscles, perhaps an exotic twist on a classic cocktail, or maybe he could convince him to try that seaweed gin.

"Yes, sir what request are you after?" Eddie smiled.

"Come on Elinee?" he smiled and walked off before Eddie could even move his face muscles.

Eddie glanced over to Jackson who would have laughed had their attention not been stolen by Josh who walked up the stairs, he made his way around the restaurant, water dripping from his soaked shirt as he went.

"I'm very sorry." He began as he looked back down to his sodden notepad, which had been obliterated by Scott's water pistol along with any notion that Josh had any idea what he was doing. Ink pooled on the paper as his order disintegrated before his eyes. He pushed his soggy hair out the way and looked the lady in her eyes, hoping she knew what she had done. "I'm sorry the chefs can't make your son a peanut butter and jam sandwich."

7:33pm

"It's just really bright." The woman said again with a small whine.

"I could bring you another chair and move you to this side of the table?" Ali smiled kindly whilst looking around the restaurant for a free chair. The ladies gluten free club in front of her had been difficult from their first step in the door.

The whole group clicked in her direction so regularly you would assume they were getting in beat for an a cappella number. Luckily if they had started singing, they would have been drowned out by Come on Elieen.

"No, I don't want to move. I'm comfortable but can you just do something about it?" the woman whined again pointing accusingly at the window.

Ali took a deep breath, feeling the need to fully clarify the request she had received. "You want me to move the sun?"

7:35pm

Josie approached the bar, placing her iPad down, bracing herself against it with her forearms. Alec sat across the bar from Eddie, wearing his usual suit and sipping a negroni.

"You alright Jose?" Eddie asked whilst pouring out two French martinis.

"Can you be honest with me?"

"Of course."

"Am I good at my job?" She asked, her eyes already searching his face for truth.

He paused his action of placing the single rose petals on top of the froth. "Of course, you are." Giving her his full attention now. "Why do you ask?"

"I just feel like everything is slipping through my fingers." She looked back at the pub, full and bustling with energy. From a glance you could see plates of well-designed food being served, empty ones taken away, laughter filled the room as did the aroma of garlic and rosemary. But if you fully gazed, fully looked, fully saw the cracks. The empty plates were sitting for a while, the people in the bar were close to seeing the bottom of their glasses, and the rosemary was only just masking the sweat of the staff.

"Maybe today is a little hectic, but don't ignore all the smooth shifts." Eddie smiled trying to reassure her. "Remember May 15th? That was a good shift."

"That's true." She nodded. "It's just… every time I walk past next door, I'm reminded they are closing… again…

has any business stayed open there for longer than six months? Are we next?"

"Jose." He leaned forward a bit, the edge of his crisp white shirt only just missing a small spill of beer on the edge of the bar. "You just need to look about to see we are doing well. We have an established reputation and clientele, and people keep coming back no matter how many times they are served by Abbie and Dan."

"If I may." Alec asked, looking at Josie with his wise kind eyes. She immediately felt a little calmer as if her grandpa had squeezed her hand and said, you are going to be ok kid.
"When I was a younger lad. My regiment was separated, dotted in the French countryside. We were found, young girl, but don't underestimate her, she got us down onto an escape line, think they called it the comet line, but there was a fair few back then and my memory isn't what it was." he paused pulling the tumbler of deep red liquid to his lips, but hastily putting it down as the story returned to him. "We heard one of our buddies had been picked up. There was no debate, we knew we had to find him, get him out of the mess." he paused again.

Eddie was suddenly distracted, noticing Josh in his peripherals as he slipped around to the back bar again, pouring another rum and coke into his bottle. He rolled his eyes, turning his attention back to Josie and Alec.

"And did you?" Josie pushed him.
"He was dead before we made it." Alec finished abruptly.

"Sometimes you do your best and it's not good enough. But you are a smart girl, you'll know what to do."

7:40pm

"Sorry." Christina said, rubbing her forehead whilst looking at Josie with a mixture of pleading and pain. Her silver pixie cut hair was slicked back as she had recently pulled her face out from under the cold water tap in the KP section. "Say it once more."

"He's allergic to nuts, garlic, onion, gluten and he's a vegetarian." Josie offered a pained smile. The kitchen had progressed in temperature from summer's day with no breeze to sauna. Josie was pulling at her shirt loosely trying to create some airflow.

"Nuts, garlic, gluten, vegetarian." Chris started again staring at the menu with more crossed out than a classified file in James Bond.

"God it's just natural selection at this point." Scott sighed from the corner where his face was pressed firmly into the wall.

7:58pm

"Where's it goin?" Abbie asked, already picking up the burger and fries sitting on the side. The restaurant was packed, as were the seats at the bar. It was clear in his step that Josh frequented the back bar more times than a small, eighteen-year-old with little experience in alcohol consumption should have.

"No, someone sent it back." Danny quickly took it out of her hands, placing it back into the side just as Bonnie Tylers holding out for a hero started for the fourth time over the speakers.

"Why? Looks fine?" Abbie tried to inspect it a little closer.

"Their candle was unlit; and they thought the oil lamp was vinegar and put it on the fries." Danny explained, trying not to laugh, Abbie also suppressed her giggling. He handed her a small empty ramekin and the squeezy bottle of ketchup for the millionth time, she turned away letting the bright red sauce splatter over the pot. Danny took it back, placing it on the side ready for Molly to swipe as she passed. He smiled down at his shirt. *Still pristine.*

Abbie looked down at the deadly seasoned chips. "Wonder how much they put on…" she mulled the thought whilst giving him a mischievous glance.

"William?" Josie asked in utter disbelief a tall gentleman in his late 50s walked in. He had a thick head of hair despite it being entirely grey, he looked as if he had just stepped out of a golf club, wearing cream chinos, a blue striped shirt and a bright pink jumper hanging over his shoulders.

Josie quickly smoothed down her hair and straightened her shirt, trying to plaster on her usual bright smile as she greeted the man whose business she was running.

"I thought you were in Switzerland?" She asked hoping she could mask her erratic stress as uncontrolled enthusiasm.

"No, I came back the other day and just thought I'd pop by." William's voice was as smooth as top shelf whisky as she casually glanced around his restaurant that he forgot existed most days.

"Yes yes, all fine here."

She was interrupted by a burst of flames followed by a large collection of gasps. Abbie and Danny stood giggling over their potato fire pit.

Josie looked back at her boss. For once very glad to see how dilated his pupils were.

08:26pm

"I don't know what to say." Scott sighed.

"Look I don't know either, but she said it's too fishy." Ali shrugged as they both looked down at the dish of Seabass staring back at them. The whole night had felt like PTSD to her trial shift, at least this time she wasn't crying.

Everyone in the kitchen looked exhausted. Ali was already sweating through her black clothes, and she had only stepped in for one complaint. Carlin sprinted from the fridge past her to his section, a trail of flour fell out his trousers as he passed. Ali looked around confused at the puddles of white powder, so much potential cake mix littering around all the men's feet. She shrugged it off. The kitchen was hotter than Mount Doom at this point.

"If I have to void it off, it'll just have to be done." Josie sighed absolutely exasperated. Her ginger hair was as messy as Abbie's and her smile all but disappeared from her face.

"Well, that was the last one I can't make another." Christina pointed at her perfectly cooked fish in pain.

Suddenly smoke poured from the other side of the kitchen. Billowing thickly from the grill as Mattie pushed it closed staggering away in a coughing fit.

"Fuckin ell Matt. We aren't calling Rohan for aid" Scott yelled.

"Who's Rohan?" Josie asked with abrupt pleading. "Can they help?"

09:09pm

"This was supposed to be here at 9am not 9pm." Danny scolded the delivery driver who held out a clipboard for Danny to sign whilst his colleague unloaded the kitchen's delivery into the entrance of the restaurant. "Why would we want a food order at 9pm on a Saturday night!" Danny exclaimed gesturing angrily at the bustling restaurant.

"Look mate, do you want it or not?" The guy shrugged, offering a pen. Danny's shoulders fell.

"Al." Danny grabbed her as she passed. She halted her power walk.

"Yup?"

"Can you sign for the delivery?" he asked, trying to hand over the clipboard.

"Why can't you?"
"ink? near this shirt? please." he scoffed, she rolled her eyes and reluctantly signed before scurrying away to the other side of the pub.

"Josh!" Danny hollered to him. Josh waddled over, very focused on putting one foot in front of the other. He reached the front door just as the last of the delivery was plonked down.

"Yup?" Josh asked as innocently as his slurring allowed.

"Never mind." Danny waved him away.

"Jackson, I need you to take this delivery down." Danny hollered, turning away from the driver abruptly bumping directly into Jackson who was already behind him. "Thank you." he said through a deep breath, containing his frustration and regaining composure.

Danny returned to the piling tickets on the rails of his section. *God it never ends.*

"Bloody relentless, isn't it?" Abbie tutted as she approached the dispense section, a large plate in one hand, and a bunch of dirty linen napkins squashed in the other. She plopped the plate down and Danny pushed it to one side, eyeing up the leftover sauce swarming around the bone of a lamb chop.

"Josh is drunk." Danny stated the obvious. "Why did you let him on the back bar tonight?" He asked unscrewing his own bottle, swigging the white wine inside. "Oh my god." he sighed as it all fell into place in his mind. "You're trying to get him fired or sent home, so Mattie doesn't win the bet?"

"It only counts if he finishes the shift." Abbie explained the rules they knew all too well.

Danny looked at her with a smile, admiring the commitment but slightly fearful at the ruthlessness.

"The way tonight is going; he will only get cut if he drops dead." Danny laughed. He looked over at Abbie who narrowed her eyes at Josh slightly. "Give up Abs."

"Giving up isn't in this season." She flicked stray hair out her face dramatically.

The lift pinged as he pulled out a large order of desserts, including one of the special Crème Brûlée. Scott had told them to sell it as a sharing dessert between two but the large round, shallow ceramic bowl looked like it could feed a small village. *Someone's overcompensating.* Danny thought, raising his eyebrows.

"Bit much, aren't they?" Abbie nodded to the huge dish; the sweet smell filled her nose as she got closer to the golden crisp layer on top. The bundle of dirty napkins tumbled out of her hands, Danny made his way around the edge of the bar to help gather them up, careful to keep the smears of a three-course meal at a distance.

"Where are they going?" Ali asked as she approached picking up Brûlée. Ali's ponytail was pulled so tight it could pass as a facelift whilst her glasses were halfway down her nose.

Danny pulled himself back up to full height, peering at the rail. "Table 31 please Al."

"Right." She turned away just as Josh stumbled past with a drink order.

Danny saw the chain of events as if they happened in slow motion, he moved fast and unapologetically.

The other three were left in shock as Josh crashed into Ali. Ali jerked backward; the dessert slid from its already precarious position on the wooden board. Danny grabbed Abbie by the shoulders, pulling her up as he ducked behind her. Ali's vain attempt at catching the dish resulted in her catapulting it directly at Abbie who stood in stunned silence as white chocolate cream splattered her torso. The only blessing that at least some fell into her mouth.

"Oh Abs!" Ali started. "I'm so sorry." She put the splattered Crème Brûlée down and turned to look for some blue roll, but Jacks was already tossing her one, lucky that the pile of delivered goods included cleaning products.

Danny carefully peered around Abbie who he still held firmly in place as a human shield.

She turned slowly to look at him.

"Abbie I just want to start by saying." he stepped away slowly as he advanced on him. "Your sacrifice is appreciated by me and my shirt..." he continued, backing away. "You have always been such a dear friend to me..." he let out a small screech before running into the washroom where Abbie didn't bother to pursue him.

She turned to Ali who held out a wad of tissue for her. Abbie started dabbing it off, the splash of white dessert dripped off her.

"You know it looks like…"
"Shut up Aioli."

09:22pm

"I can see a table right there." The gentleman at the door exclaimed, frustrated, pointing at a table which was due to be filled in the next ten minutes.

"I'm sorry sir but that's booked very soon."

"Well can't you move them somewhere else?" He tutted.

Josie looked about the restaurant. She looked at her building. Her staff. Her life.

Operatic music began to blare, and she felt the moment stretch into slow motion. A bottle of champagne lost control in Eddie's hand, the cork shooting straight into Jacksons chest who collapsed out of view behind the bar.

"Zanahoria!" he yelled but to Josie it was just a faint noise lost amongst the chaos.

Abbie and Danny were engaged in a heated conversation, gestures wide and aggressive.

She carried on turning her head catching the moment Josh's finger slipped whilst opening a bottle of red wine tableside. The small blade used to peel back the foil sliced across his palm as he held it out gushing in front of him., face twisted in horror as he wasn't sure whether to finish opening the bottle or bleed out in the middle of the restaurant.

Scott was at the top of the stairs, waving a ticket in Ali's face who was rocking back and forth with her hands over her ears.

All her senses snapped back into action.

"Right!" she declared, turning back to the gentleman at the door. "Sorry we don't have a table so please leave." She said with an air of finality. The gentleman recoiled in horror, clearly unaccustomed to not getting his way.

Josie found a spare chair, placing it in the center of the restaurant and hoisted herself up.

"Deepest apologies everyone but we are closing now." She announced loudly. All chatter stopped as they looked up to her. "We have run out of food and the will to carry on, so once you have finished your drinks and food kindly pay and vacate the building. If you are unhappy, as I am sure most of you are, I shall be by the door to receive complaints. And whichever of my staff members has hacked the sound system, please put on an appropriate song." Josie got off her chair and readied herself at the door.

This must be how it feels to stand in front of a firing squad. She thought, wishing she was allowed a blindfold and a fast way out of the situation.

"Hit the road Jack. don't you come back no more no more no more no more." Ray Charles appeared over the restaurant to support her decision just as the first disgruntled patron approached her.

10:00pm

The final notes of goodnight sweetheart played as the last customers filtered out the door.

The chefs had been lounging in the corner of the restaurant, each with a glass of water in front of them.

Josie marched over to the door and clapped her hands. She pulled the pub keys out her pocket and put it in the lock.

The whole team looked at each other in shock. Like zombies rising from the dead with no urgent purpose to pursue, they all stood and silently congregated in the space between the bar and the restaurant.

"You are either in or out." Josie stated hand firmly on the key ready and raring to begin the lock in.

Welcome to the Bells

Volume 5

"Ground Rules!" Eddie clapped to get the attention of the team as they pulled together tables and chairs getting settled for the night. "No one but myself or Jacks behind the bar. Nothing top shelf and no double parking." Everyone nodded in agreement as they waited eagerly for their drinks which Jackson was already preparing.

The carnage of the service began to melt away as Jackson placed down everyone's drinks in front of them.

"Thanks Jacks." Danny nodded as he was passed a gin and tonic.

Jackson gave a small bow of appreciation.

"You are off the clock, you know Jacks?" Josie gestured to the empty restaurant.

Jackson pointed to the roof before shaking their head.

"I forgot under the roof still counts." Josie apologised sipping a glass of wine so large it didn't just ignore the weights and measures act but blew it up and buried the remains.

Everyone hummed in agreement whilst Josh looked between them all in confusion. Normally he would have let confusion wash over and stay on the outside, but Josh had already been drinking since the beginning of service which gave him the confidence of a regular 18-year-old.

"What counts for what?" He stammered out the sentence, he felt all their eyes descend.

"Did you guys do not tell Josh?" Matteo laughed through a long gulp of beer.

"Of course, we did…" Ali started trailing off as she saw the rest of the front of house team shaking their heads. "Not. We did not." She finished sipping her drink, cheeks turning slightly red in embarrassment. Matteo rolled his eyes at them all and turned to Josh.

"Well Cole bet Jackson that they couldn't do their job without talking." he explained, and Jackson nodded.
"Who is Cole?" Josh asked, looking around for someone he didn't recognise.

"He was a waiter here before he left for uni." Matt explained.

"He graduates in a couple of weeks." Josie smiled.

"Good for him." Scott let out a small laugh, he pulled out his wallet and passed a note over to Christina.

"Do you guys bet on everything?" Josh asked, not shocked in the slightest.

"Pretty much." Abbie shrugged, finishing her drink just as Eddie sat down.
He looked at her with a mixture of awe and fear before getting back up to make her another.

"What do you guys bet?" Josh asked, shuffling his chair closer, fully ready to enter the inner circle.

"Depends how high stakes it is." Abbie shrugged. "We bet on things like trading sections, trading bad customers, bad close down jobs or if you are really confident closing times."

"Remember when Ali…" Danny trailed off already laughing.

"Yeah, I know." She snapped. "My three-hour delivery shift changed into a 2am close." She explained to Josh whilst glaring at Danny and Abbie who sipped their drinks with no shame.

"Oh." Josie looked slightly wounded. "I thought you were just really committed."

"Oh I am." Ali slid her hand across the table to reassure her. "Just not that much." She finished patting Josies hand.

Scott looked amongst his chefs proudly. "Well, my team are-

"Oh, shut the fuck up." Josie cut him off. Everyone stopped dead silent looking at their leader. Aggression looked stranger on Josie than number 10 did on Boris Johnson. Eddie took it as his cue to start repouring another round.

"Is this what you have been fighting about?" Danny asked.

Josh nudged Ali next to him. "They have been fighting?" He mumbled.

"Scott here, thinks that we don't work hard!" Josie snapped. The flood gates had opened as suppressed fury bubbled up faster than a mento in a coke bottle.
"That's not what I said or meant, and you know it!" he

leant forward to defend himself.

"Just that up here takes no skill. That's what you meant wasn't it."

"Well a little yes. Anyone can just become a front of house staff... no offence Josh." Scott finished sending an apologetic glance to Josh.

"Not everyone can be good at it though. Same way anyone can walk into a kitchen but not everyone can make a half decent *omelette*."

"Come on you know-

"No, I am sick of you belittling what we do up here." She cut him off. "You wouldn't last a day up here!"

"Easily!" He scoffed.

"Anything you can do, we can do better!" Abbie spoke, being the first to step up in defense despite taking her job least seriously.

"Please don't start singing." Matteo sighed.

"I'm being serious. What we do up here is difficult" she looked about at her friends who all nodded in agreement.

"Not like being in the kitchen." He snorted which was followed by a series of nods from his team.

"Stop being so self-important. You lot wouldn't last an hour up here." she snapped.

"Wanna bet?" Matt shot back, he stood up abruptly, hand already out ready to shake on a deal.

"No!" Josie stepped in. "I am NOT staffing my restaurant with chefs."

"We settle this now then!" Abbie slammed her glass down, standing up to face Matt, their noses were inches away, both looked ready to vault the table ready to fight for the honour of their team.

"Back of House versus front of house. Each side picks skills to test and nominate a team member." Matt began laying down the rules. "Can't nominate the same person twice." he quickly added, not wanting to come up against Eddie more than once.

"What do you win?" Josh asked, getting more invested by the second.

"Pride!" They both snapped synchronised. The pair of them shook hands fiercely and straightened up, ready for battle.

"Ok then Mattie." Abbie let the decision of round one fall to her opponents. "What can you do that we can't?"

He sipped his beer and chuckled. "Knife skills." He said easily and the kitchen team all let out a communal sigh of relief. Clearly believing a point in their favour already.

"Agreed." Abbie nodded. "And who do you nominate?"

The chefs all looked around themselves nodding in agreement as Christina stood up.

"And you?" Mattie asked.

"Give me two minutes." Eddie called from behind the bar.

"How about we make this a productive bet?" Josie suggested.

11:00pm

The whole team stood in the kitchen. Front of house peeling potatoes ready for Sunday roast. Thomas making batter for Yorkshire puddings. Carlin and Jasmine prepped vegetables.

"Ok." Josie resided as mediator for the first challenge. "Whoever does prep the fastest wins."

Eddie and Christina stood over uncut herbs, whole lemons and limes, and a small selection of peeled potatoes ready for chopping. Both knives had been sharpened by Matteo. the selection of items selected and weighed out by Abbie. Both kitchen and bar prep, ready to be raced against.

Christina flexed her shoulders and corrected her stance ready. Whilst Eddie twisted his wrists and got used to the weight and size of the knife.

"Three. Two. One." Josie counted. "GO!"

Josh looked away feeling dizzy at the speed of the movement in front of him. He focused his vision on the cold tap in the sink trying not to fall over. He wanted to keep up the pace of his colleagues. Finally feeling like one of the team. Throwing up now would be like flushing the key to the castle down the toilet. But he couldn't admit he had been drinking nearly five hours longer than everyone else.

There was an abrupt eruption of applause. Josh turned round to see Eddie casually spinning the knife in his hand, pausing to blow the leftover herbs off the tip, like a cowboy blowing the smoke from his pistol.

Christina finished her prep before nodding at Eddie in respect.

11:30pm

"Ok then." Matteo shrugged off the loss. "Next challenge."

The whole team remained in the kitchen. everyone had been given a job. Whether cling filming fruit, washing up, chopping vegetables, prepping meat, stirring whatever handed to them, polishing cutlery or bringing down more drinks. The whole team was put to use.

"You need a good Memory." Abbie grinned from a gleaming set of steak knives.

"Agreed. Nomination?" Matteo accepted the challenge.

"Ali?" Abbie offered. Ali turned away from the sink accepting the challenge.

"Jas?" Mattie called who looked up from a pile of vegetables.

"Two parts to the test. You have to memorise two orders. Drinks and food. Whoever can repeat them back most accurately wins." Abbie laid the rules.

11:55pm

"Sorry guys." Ali said whilst looking down at her feet.

"You said medium not medium rare." Abbie reassured her as they climbed the stairs. "Hardly a loss." she squeezed her friend's shoulder.

"Still a loss!" Matteo called from the back of the group.

They all settled back into the plush chairs of the restaurant as Eddie began to make the next round of drinks.

"Ok, what's the third challenge?" Danny urged the conversation on from front of house defeat.

Everyone looked about wondering.

"I got one." Carlin spoke up. Josh was surprised at how high his voice was, once again urging the thought at how the boy was allowed to drink, let alone how he could hold his liquor better than most at the table. "You've got to have good strength and stamina." Carlin suggested.

"Good old fashioned arm wrestling." Matteo said, smacking his hand onto the table, feeling another point on his score board already. "Thomas! Step up dear boy." Mattie moved out the way to give their tribute centre stage. Abbie cleared the way for Jackson to take the space opposite.

Both sides eyed each other skeptical of their decisions. Thomas being a lanky tall pastry chef, more hair than muscle. He tightened his bun before taking a seat steadying his arm ready on the table. Jackson rolled up their sleeves, locking hands.

"Three." Scott began the countdown. "Two. One. GO!"

12:30am

"I have one." Josie interjected slurring her words but in a way that was ever so slightly classy. Thomas and Jackson remained casually locked in battle as neither shifted which had led to a very uneventful half hour and another round of drinks.

"Product knowledge." Josie suggested the next challenge.

"Come on then Jose." Scott stood up before anyone else could even think. "Let's have a quiz."

01:05am

"Think we need to call it a stalemate." Matteo finally interrupted as they had both correctly listed every dish served since the opening, the gin taste test had been equal along with the naming of every ingredient in the bouillabaisse sauce, even every wine pairing had been deemed equally correct.

"Ok, deciding round." Abbie stood up, commanding the attention of the whole room. "We can all agree that teamwork is the foundation of what we all do?" She looked around at the shared nods and smiles. "That the shared experience within the building and the bonds we make are a huge part of the success behind the business. The social challenges extend far beyond the team as well, we make every customer feel special, we create rapport with the suppliers, we keep each other sane." She continued whilst elevating her voice and even eliciting a cheer from Josie. "So, I challenge you." She continued pointing directly at Matteo. "To name one thing you know about us."

"What?" He laughed in disbelief. "One thing?"

"One thing about each of us. And you win." Abbie sat down looking smug. Matt laughed again and looked around.

"Well Ali is doing a degree in overthinking." He began.

"Philosophy, but same difference." She corrected. "And I have technically finished it now."

"Josie has been in hospitality since she was fifteen." He continued. His gaze settled on Abbie and Danny but moved on to buy more time.

"Eddie is Italian." he spoke proudly. "Josh is... young." he trailed off and blew out his breath getting increasingly frustrated. His eyes settled for a moment on Jackson but realising he was unsure even on their first name, so he moved on. Matt took a long sip of his beer in an attempt to buy him time. The rest of the chefs gave small shrugs, ensuring he at least wasn't lost alone.

"Well, you don't know us either!" He snorted defensively. Abbie lent back and cracked her knuckles before sipping her cider.

"Where to start." She sighed. "Scott is an only child, he started cooking when he was thirteen and went to culinary school before starting off in an Asian restaurant, his favourite drink is a mojito, but he drinks beer because he wants to fit in. Jas is Somali, she moved to England with her family as a child and has worked her way up since the age of sixteen. Chris is the youngest of five, she loves history, especially Vikings, probably due to her Norwegian heritage and growing up there. Thomas began making desserts for his school fairs as a child, he made so much money he started doing it for charity before realising it could be a career, he has been with his girlfriend for seven years, and is thinking of proposing soon. Carlin is still in college, he's a part time chef and full time Emo." Abbie took a sip of her drink triumphantly before slowly sitting down, leaning back in her chair with ease. "As just proven, you guys know nothing about us." Abbie smirked.

"He knew something." Christina defended her teammate.

Jackson rolled their eyes and pointed to Eddie.

"That's true." Eddie mused. "You don't even know where I am from."

"You are from Italy."

"No, I'm Greek." He corrected. "I studied in Italy."

"I thought you were Spanish?" Danny looked quizzically at him.

"No, he worked in Spain for a couple years." Abbie corrected and Eddie shared a moment of pleasant surprise that someone actually listened to him.

"Paris for a bit too." He smiled at good memories.

"So how many languages do you speak?" Matteo asked.

"Six and a bit." He smiled. "Unless you include computer languages then nine and a bit."

"What's the bit?" Ali asked.

"BSL."

"You know how to program?" Matteo blinked.

"I started off working as a software engineer in Greece. My father runs a company. But it wasn't very social, and I wanted to travel, so I went to Italy and studied languages. Worked at a bar in my free time. I realised I loved it. And it seems alcohol consumption is one thing most of the world agrees with. So, I started travelling as a bartender." He finished by taking a long-satisfied sip of a cocktail that definitely wasn't on the menu.

"So, what are all the other languages?" Christina asked, resting her elbows on the edge of the table, listening intently.

"Greek, Italian, Spanish, French, English and Russian."

"You worked in Russia?"

"No, I just thought it would come in handy if there is a new world war." He shrugged.

"What about you Jacks?" Thomas asked, deflecting the topic to his equal in arm-wrestling.

Everyone looked expectantly as they pulled a napkin from the centre of the table where the place settings had been pushed together in a mound that looked like a tomorrow problem. Holding out an open palm to Ali who pulled a black pen from her ponytail, they looked to Josie who nodded indifferently to the artistic vandalism on her white linen.

Everyone watched intently as Jackson began to scribble. After a few moments of uneventful spectating, they all simultaneously agreed to leave the artist at work.

"Josh is going to do a Physics degree." Abbie boasted on his behalf whilst he went red in the cheeks, partly embarrassed, but also nervous as he wondered how she had got such information.

"Really?" Scott asked wide eyed.

"Is that really that surprising?" Josh stuttered not sure where to look with all eyes on him.

"Always had you pegged as a film student or something."

The conversation moved on into friendly chatter as everyone found new interest in the people they shared most of their lives with.

"Hey, what about us?" Abbie protested, gesturing dramatically to herself and Danny.
"What about you?" Matt shrugged. "You're like us. in it for the long haul." He wrote them off as committed to the industry, clearly ignoring the consistent laissez faire attitude they bring to every shift. Josie let out a short snort before coughing out an apology.

"We are artists as well!" She proclaimed proudly whilst standing up to display her best side. "I'll have you know I am a fully trained actor and singer."
"No dancing?" Matt laughed.

"Please Darling, other people need hope." she flicked her hair.

"What about you Danny? you dance?"

"Only to the Spice Girls." He said putting down his drink and leaning forward. "I am a writer."
"Really?" Matt's eyes widened in interest. "Books? scripts? plays?"

"Yes."

"What about you Al?" Thomas asked. Eddie pulled himself up to start making another drink for Ali as the existential crisis built behind her eyes.

"Well, I don't know." She admitted finishing off her drink plonking it on the table just in time for Eddie to clear it and give her a fresh one.

"You are young." Jasmine assured her. "You have time."

"You don't have to choose your life right now." Christina smiled. "I was training to be a surgeon for a while." Everyone stared in confusion, even Matteo and Thomas looked on in shock. "Changed my career because I was too stressed."

"In your less stressful plan you went with being a chef?"

"Still an adrenaline rush, just no one's life on the line." She shrugged. "Unless someone forgets to mention a nut allergy." She glared threateningly at the front of house team.

Everyone splits into their own conversations. Josie fell into an engaged discussion with Chris about her time in medicine, whilst the boys of the kitchen were wrapped in Eddie's stories from the continent. Ali was listening to

Scott thoughtfully, whilst Jackson continued to sketch on napkins.

On the other side of the table Abbie felt as if everything she even hoped for was out of her grasp. it had melted away to nothing without her even realising.

Where did it all go?

"What's up?" Danny sensed something wrong, turning fully toward her, his eyes looking deep into her lost expression.

"I don't remember the last audition I went for?" she sighed, and looked away, down into her half empty gin. "When did I stop?" she looked more intently at the clear liquid in the large bowl glass, as if it were a mirror to the past where she could pinpoint the date of her last self-tape. "When did I stop acting?" She asked looking up to Danny now as if he had the answer.

"You still act." he spoke gently, putting a hand on her shoulder. "You act like you care every day." she gave him a playful shove but couldn't conceal the smile.

"I'm serious." she said, her smile going limp on her lips. "How did I give up and not realise?" She looked at him for an answer.

"Maybe you just needed a break." He offered. "You can go back to it whenever you want."

"You know I'm not sure I can. I've forgotten what the rejection feels like and waiting to expect bad news but then keep waiting and receive nothing. I'm not sure I've got it in me anymore." She looked away from him back to her drink. His hand slid naturally into hers, a firm squeeze pulled her attention back to him.

"If you want it, it's yours." Danny's smile was kind, full belief sitting behind it. "You're braver than you believe." She gave a small snort. "Who said that?"
"Winnie the Pooh." they laughed between themselves. Abbie let her head flop onto his shoulder, and he put his arm firmly around her.

1:34am

Josh appeared at the top of the stairs. Still buttoning up his jeans.

"My trial shift really was that bad." Ali finished her story as the whole room erupted into laughter.

Oh, for fuck's sake.

1:47am

"You know guys." Josie sat up addressing them all. "Sometimes I play Candy Crush on the iPad."

02:16am

Abbie and Danny finished their curtain call as Ali's solitary applause echoed through the empty pub. The rest of the audience grimaced, not sure how to respond to the sudden, but somehow well-rehearsed performance of defying gravity. Most of them couldn't fathom why Abbie, a trained performer, would concede the lead role to Danny but friendship is all about giving away first place even if ice in a blender would have been a more appealing sound.

"Sorry I asked." Matt sighed, having instantly regretted mentioning he had never been to the theatre despite being a London resident for long enough.

3:00am

"Dam Jacks." Christina exclaimed, pulling one of the now many doodles toward her. "This is us." She pointed at the comic like sketches. Christina and Matteo's bet of who can finish a pint faster, forever immortalised in black ink on a crisp white napkin.

Thomas pulled one from the growing pile toward him. Holding it up next to the slouched figure of Carlin fast asleep, curled up like a cat in a chair.

"You want to be an artist?" he asked.

Jackson nodded, pushing the most recent piece toward him, he studied it. Ali and Scott clinking glasses at the other end of the table.

3:57am

"And there you have it." Eddie said simply.

"Ok so it was mierda, verpiss dich, merde, fanculo and.." he trailed off copying the signs Eddie had just shown him.

"You got it." He smiled feeling that he had passed on wisdom, the way a father might teach his son how to fix a bike tyre. "You can now swear in 6 languages."

4:20am

Matteo, Josh and Carlin filed back inside laughing, smelling pungent and smokey.

"That's absolutely mental." Matt laughed with Carlin as Josh nodded.
"I shit you not." He carried on. "Every decision we make could be split into a new universe."
"How do we get there?" Carlin asked, fully invested. "Is there a universe where My Chemical Romance never broke up?"
"Probably." Josh shrugged.

Josie sniffed the air from her relaxed slump in one of the nicer chairs from the tables they only give to regulars. She took a sip of her wine and shrugged off the smell, putting it down to the sage she was burning before service began.

5:39am

"Who am I?" Josh asked.

"That's not how you play the game, alright?" Mattie spoke in his best attempt an Italian could make of Birmingham accent. "It's called identity theft for a reason."

"Who am I?" He asked again.

"You got your piece of paper, right?" Christina nodded to the small slip torn from a note pad in his hand. "You just have to act like whoever is on it. If someone guesses who you are, you and that person dish out forfeit drinks." Jackson shifted wincing as they did, everyone watched slightly confused before moving on.

"But you can't just say who you are. You just have to adopt quirks or say things they might say."

"Ja!" Danny chimed in, putting on the thickest German accent he could. No one said a thing despite it being obvious he was the most famous German, who was actually Austrian.

"Who am I?" Josh repeated.

"I thought I made them pretty easy or at least within the scope of the interests of people here." Josie defended choices of names she had put in the hat, as she sat on the sidelines enjoying the role play. Jackson shifted again awkwardly, putting on a wince as they did.

"Exactly." Abbie said, putting her sunglasses on. "We got a mystery to solve." She finished pulling them off again slowly whilst looking off into the distance.

Again, a couple of them contemplated before moving on.

Matteo got up and walked behind the bar, pulling a cheap bottle of whisky and coming back round. He plonked himself down pouring a small amount.

"Understand yet?" He tried again at the accent, gesturing with his whisky.

"Another mystery to solve." Abbie said putting on and pulling off her glasses in the same sentence. "What the fuck is Matties accent?" She finished by putting them back on and staring back off into the distance.

"Ja unlike mine ja?" Danny urged them all to guess.

Eddie pulled a napkin from the table that Jackson had not claimed as a canvas. Tying it into a ball he held it above his head before throwing it perfectly into the bin.

"Michel Jordan!" Thomas jumped to his feet. Even though he wasn't assuming a character himself his guess was correct, and they both delegated their forfeits to Abbie and Mattie.

Jackson shifted and winced again.

"Well Jack's has clearly got something up their arse." Jasmine laughed.

"Scott!" Abbie yelled and Jackson smiled, confirming her triumph, dishing out shots to Scott and Josie.

"Thanks Jose." Scott said through gritted teeth as he winced away the tequila.

"It's Jackson's interpretation not mine."

"That's right boss." Mattie continued, adding more threat to his gestures.

"Are you a mob boss Mattie?" Molly asked.

"Gotta be more specific darlin." He tried to make his voice a little deeper.

"Mob bosses are my specialty." Abbie spoke slowly, taking off her glasses one more time.

"You are one of those CSI guys!" Thomas said excitedly, clicking his figures, waiting for the exact name to come to his mind.

"Yes!" Abbie cheered, slamming a shot in front of Matteo.

"If I gotta be specific then so does she." He protested breaking character.

Abbie flipped over the paper in front of her to reveal in Josie's handwriting *one of those CSI guys.*

"Fair enough!" He receded.

"Who am I?" Josh continued tugging at the same string, adding a slight musical tone to his voice.

"Someone with amnesia?" Christina shrugged.

Matteo pulled out every trick he could. Bringing a bottle of gin into the equation, talking of family, stealing Chris' cap and Danny's coat.

"You better fuckin guess soon." He said menacingly.

"Who am I?" Josh asked again this time adding a French accent.

Abbie stood up ready to shout, finger already out-stretched in Josh's direction. "YOU'RE JEAN VAL JEAN!"

Matteo threw the hat to the floor. "I'm Thomas fuckin Shelby!"

"Oh, I see it now." Ali whispered to Danny.

7:30am

The tinkle of a phone going off. Everyone looked about wondering who would be calling in the middle of the night. Everyone started shifting through the mess to find the source.

"It's mine guys." Christina admitted. "It's my alarm though."

"Scheisse!" Danny cursed.

"It's ok Danny, you can drop the accent, we all know you're Hitler." Ali finally released him from the game.

"It can't be morning?" Josie sighed in disbelief before moving to pull back the curtain and sure enough the slow light of dawn poured in, a wave of moans rippled through the room.

"Ok anyone is welcome to come back and shower at mine." Offered Scott and a couple of the chefs nodded thanks and got ready to follow their leader home to his power shower and vast range of soaps.

"Ok everyone home and I'll see you back in a few hours." Josie started the sentence with a smile and ended looking ready to cry.

"I'll lock up Jose." Danny smiled sleepily from where he was slouched.

"Are you sure?" She asked slowly whilst sliding on her coat and glancing under furniture for her bag.

"Yeah, I got this." Danny reassured whilst the rest of the team reluctantly climbed to their feet.

"I'm already not expecting a good service tomorrow. I'll just be happy if everyone turns up." She said whilst holding the door open for them all to file out.

"Don't worry about us Jose." Scott started. "Downstairs we will be fine, one thing back of house definitely wins at, is handling hangovers."

She rolled her eyes, whilst memorising the exact wording ready to throw back at him if he starts crying into Yorkshire puddings.

Abbie stayed behind with Danny; they plonked a few glasses on the edge of the bar before tucking a few chairs away. Making a small attempt to make their mornings easier.

"Jacks is bloody good." Danny laughed, spreading out the napkin gallery to view each masterpiece properly. It was like looking back at the night through a linen comic book.

"Yeah, not bad at all." Abbie agreed. Pulling a napkin depicting Eddie teaching Thomas how to waltz. Danny tugged at one from the bottom of the pile, showing the beginning of the night when Carlin was still sober enough to do card tricks.

He looked over to Abbie as she let out a small chuckle. The corners of her eyes crinkled with a smile as she pushed one over to him.

"We put on a great show, don't we?" She laughed at the sketch of them standing over a couple of tables which had made their precarious stage.

"You put on a great show." He corrected.

"Well, you make me look better."

"My sole purpose in life."

She laughed again but her smile fell slightly as she thought back to their conversation earlier.

"You don't think I've given up do you?" She asked him sincerely.

He smiled, putting an arm around her shoulders, staring down at the drawings of the night together.

"Giving up isn't in this season."

"Who said that?"

"You did. About 10 hours ago."

Abbie laughed, putting both arms around his waist. Danny shifted his body around so he could put his other arm around her. His chin rested on her head; her face pushed into his still clean, still ridiculous shirt.

They pulled apart slightly, holding one another not quiet at arm's length. Smiling. The morning sun, peeping through hit Abbies hair, making the stray stands more obvious but also highlighting its chocolate colour. It shone onto one side of Danny's face, showing his smile, so soft and safe. They stood together in the warm light of dawn, feeling full and content.

Every relationship has its boundaries. Invisible lines in the sand that say how close you can get. Some draw the line before physical contact but after you can call me if your cat died. Others are between I'll lend you a book but won't text back for 3 -5 business days. A few stands between I'll hold your hand at the doctors but not check the lump myself.

Abbie and Danny's line was so close, they were almost toe to toe.

Neither knew who moved first. Maybe it was just as synchronised as they had always been.

But on that Sunday morning, in the empty pub, together they stepped over their line.

Welcome to the Bells

Volume 6

"What a mess!"

Jackson paused polishing glasses to raise their eyebrows at Eddie's statement, needing him to elaborate as nearly everything that Sunday morning could be described as a mess. The tables were still littered with empty pizza boxes. Random straws and limes scattered around the dirty wooden floor. The place settings looked drunk as they had been knocked about and someone needed to wipe the footprints off the sofas.

"Look at my stock!" he pointed aggressively at the space under the ice wells where the spare spirits were kept. Jackson shrugged at the empty shelf.

"Exactly!" He exclaimed, throwing his arms out. "It's all gone!" he started massaging his temples and taking a breath. Jackson walked over to him, putting a hand on his shoulder, giving him a small smile. "You're right, it was a great night. I'll calm down." Jackson put the gleaming wine glass and polishing cloth into his hands and turned to walk away. "Te Amo Zanahoria. Four of each house spirit please!" he shouted, and Jacks threw their thumb up before trotting down the stairs.

"Do you really need to shout?" Ali winced, holding her head whilst shuffling slowly in through the front door. She looked like a celebrity... who was hiding from the paparazzi after a long night of bad decisions. Her nose looked like it was struggling to hold up the size of her sunglasses, underneath the cap her hair was wet and matted. Her outfit spoke volumes and what it said was I haven't done laundry.

"Come on Al you are young, young people are supposed to bounce back."

She made sure to pull off her large sunglasses so she could look Eddie in the eye whilst she told him to "Fuck off."

"Morning Al." Josie sprung up the stairs fresh as a daisy amongst a pile of shit. "If I knew a Hangover would get you to work on time, I would have gotten you drunk a long time ago."

Ali turned to Josie who was now next to her, iPad in hand, looking like someone who hadn't left here only a few hours prior. Josie wasn't wearing one of her signature long floral skirts but instead a light blue pair of skinny jeans with a pastel purple shirt.

"With deepest respect Josie, Fuck off." Ali pushed her glasses back on before she began a slow descent down to the staff room.

Josie and Eddie shared a look of suppressed laughter from their superior position of being functional.

Josie went and pulled open the two large windows, letting in a welcome gust of fresh air and took away the lingering stench of spilt spirits, sweat and bad decisions. Eddie took off his bow tie and undid his top button before turning back to his bar sighing once more before rolling up his sleeves.

Josie was busying herself with straightening up the place settings, whilst Eddie and Jackson were unloading a crate of spirits when Abbie strode in. She wasn't walking with her usual swagger; her clothes were fresh as was her face.

"Sorry I'm a bit late." Abbie called in Josie's direction. The three of them all perked up, jaws slightly open. They watched in silence as she descended the stairs.

Josie looked in disbelief at Eddie and Jackson. "What happened last night?"

Abbie slumped down the stairs and threw her bag in the staff room before heading to the ladies room.

It stank of cheap air freshener. The walls were a deep burgundy, the lighting so minimalistic it was close to non-existent. The cubicle doors were a deep redwood, opposite them were two gleaming white sinks.

She pulled the taps hard, shoving her wrists under the cold water. Looking up at the oval mirror into her reflection she felt a disconnect from the image of her own face. for once she had washed her hair, but it still pinged out her bun in awkward tufts. She hated her long nose and wished her cheeks weren't so round. She had spent most of the morning staring at the mirror wondering what to do. Looking at Josie's number on her phone, ready to call in sick, looking at Danny's next to it wanting to call him.

She felt sick with anticipation. wanted to run straight forward into whatever mess the two of them had created whilst at the same time turn away, turn her back and forget it happened.

But. in the moment. In the moment it was perfect. Like two puzzle pieces that had been sat next to each all of a sudden slotting. Only hours ago, she had felt dizzy with happiness, she had felt almost overwhelmed with feeling. He had held her so close, but she remembered the look on his face when the bubble had burst. The sun had been bright by that point, making his hair look even lighter. He didn't say anything out loud, but it was clear in his eyes, he was thinking of Becca.

Abbie felt on the edge of a cliff, unsure which way the wind might push.

It has been so easy before yesterday. She craved what they had before, the goodbye hugs seconds longer than what they gave to others, the gentle shoves because they could say the worst to each other knowing it would mean nothing, the smiles between shared secrets. but at the same time, she longed for more, to be honest, to be open, be everything and more.

 She felt like she was being torn apart, ripped in two directions of want and need. *Everything is going to be fine.*

"Everything is going to be…"

She was interrupted by a sound that no writer wants to attempt to explain, following a toilet flush Abbie watched the door in disgusted suspense as Ali took a little too long to emerge from the cubicle. She hobbled over to the adjacent sink with no acknowledgement that anyone was sharing the room with her. Ali put her hands under the cold water. The only sound was the cool liquid hitting the basin.

"You good?" Abbie asked with raised brows, breaking the silence. "Tactical chunder?"
Ali shook her hair slowly, her blond hair flopping still slightly wet around her face.

"I wish I could say there were any tactics involved." She said whilst bracing herself against the bowl of the sink. Abbie took a small step back out of the splash zone, but Ali let out a deep breath and straightened up. "I'm good." she announced unconvincingly.

Ali was a close friend. It was difficult to work in a restaurant without becoming bonded with your colleagues in a deep intense way. You share every weekend with them, you have their backs and they have yours, you laugh at the constant stupidity of the people you serve. But with Ali it was more, they shared more. Abbie thought about when she helped check if it really was a lump Molly had found, and when Molly bailed her out of a bad date with an 'emergency'.

Abbie took a moment, but this was going to be her only moment.
"I gotta talk to you." She spoke urgently.
Ali's eyes widened. "Fuck. What did I do last night?" Her face panicked as her brain scrambled through memories more shattered than her dignity.
"No, no, I did something." Abbie reassured quickly and Ali's face relaxed only slightly whilst shaking her head.
"Oh Jesus I don't want to know. I want plausible deniability." Ali started to walk away but was pulled back by Abbie's desperate grasp.
"Come on Mols. I need you now." she pleaded. Her large grey eyes begging whilst strengthening her grip on her friend's hand. Ali stopped. Abbie had used Molly's real name, which meant this was serious.
"What did you do?" Ali felt her stomach flip, whether a hangover or that Abbie just admitted she needed her, but she could see the desperation. She put her other hand into

Abbies and turned fully toward her giving her a light squeeze. "Abs whatever happened it's going to be ok."

Ali looked at her expectantly. Her eyes were kind and patient, and Abbie couldn't hold her gaze, Abbie hadn't thought this far in her plan, she hadn't thought much further than turning up at work. She took a deep breath and tried to pull a sentence together.

"You can't judge me." Abbie started feeling in need of a tactical chunder herself. "You can't tell anyone either."

"Abbie, you know I'm not a good liar if the police ask, I'll probably have to tell 'em something." Ali started looking slightly concerned.

"It's about Danny." Abbie started and Ali's face fell faster than Abbie could catch it.

"Is that why he hasn't come in yet? Oh, Abbie what happened? Tell me it was an accident."

"What the fuck! No!"

"You did it on purpose?" Ali pulled away.

"We slept together!" Abbie furiously whispered.

"Oh shit!

"I know I don't know what to do." She spluttered. her eyes filling with tears now, she blinked them away determined not to cry. Looking down at her feet as if the answer were in her muddy doc martens. She kept her hand firmly in Ali's as if to let go would mean to crumble.

She took a deep breath and then another. She would not break, she would not cry, especially for something as in control as her future.

"It'll be ok." Ali spoke with absolute certainty. "We can figure this out together."

"Ok team" Scott started the briefing looking around. Ali had put her glasses back on, Josh was white as a sheet, clinging to the end of the bar which seemed to be the only thing holding him up right. Danny had yet to appear. "We have a fully booked Sunday lunch, normal Sunday menu, but we have a plum crumble to sell as a special for seven pounds. We don't have much red wine jus. Can you guys send down some coffee? I'm going to send up some bacon sandwiches, let's all just try our best." he gave everyone a reassuring smile and left.

"So as Scott just said we are fully booked. I want Abbie on the front section, Molly at the back, Josh you can cover drinks. Danny will be on dispense. We have lots of large family groups in. don't stress about mistakes, do your best. Get some coffee down you before the buggies and screaming children turn up." Ali and Josh let out a pained groan, Josie gave them all a smile and left. Everyone dispersed but Abbie, she stayed glued to the end of the bar staring at the door. Danny isn't here. Maybe that was for the best. She wasn't even sure what she would say to him.

"Eddie." Abbie called.

"What do you need?" he asked not looking over but chopping limes into perfectly equal wedges.
"Bloody Mary please."
"Virgin Mary?" He looked up with slightly raised eyebrows and tried to correct her.
"Did I stutter?" She raised her eyebrow back at him.

He held up his hands in surrender. Abbie let her head fall onto the end of the bar. Her stomach twisted and not in the same way most others were that morning. Danny hadn't come in yet. Maybe he wouldn't. Maybe he couldn't face her. Or anyone. Maybe he was already with Rebecca confessing and asking for forgiveness.

Her train of thought was swiftly interrupted by a tall glass of bright red liquid. It had two straws protruding from between the ice, a lemon wedge placed next to a stick of celery and a rolled-up peel of cucumber impaled on a cocktail stick. Before tasting it, Abbie could already smell the perfectly seasoned pepper and tabasco.
"I hope you know I'm not tipping you?" she said after one sip in which the double shot of vodka kicked the back of her throat. Eddie gave her a smile and a wink. she must have looked rougher than she thought.

Abbie started absent-mindedly making coffees for all the chefs, latte for Scott and Jasmine, iced for Chris, mocha for Carlin, double espresso for Matteo and black for Thomas. Once she had the side of the counter looking like a promotional shot for caffeine, she called up the lift, hearing the slow clunking sound as it ascended.

"Danny, did you sort that inquiry about the wheelchair?" Josie called. Hearing his name Abbie turned around to see him coming up the stairs. His blond hair was a matted mess and his posture slumped; he had traded his fancy shirt for a navy t-shirt with Shakespeare on it saying he put the lit in literature. Danny was even wearing his thin framed glasses that he thought didn't suit him.

"Sorry I just got off the phone with the eight-dog lady. I'll go sort it." He called back in a flat tone.

Abbie watched him as he turned to descend back to the office. She wanted to say anything, do anything, wanted to let him know she was still here. She froze up just watching.

He stopped and turned back to her. She felt her whole-body jolt. He smiled, it was small and tired, but it was there. She felt her heart rate being too slow. *Everything will be ok; we will sort it out.* He turned away, carrying on down the stairs and disappearing from view.

"Thanks for doing that, Abbie." Josie snapped Abbie back, nodding at the coffees. "Could you change the tills for Sunday roasts to be available please?"

"Yeah, no problem." She muttered back before sending them down in the lift.

Josie shared a confused glance with Jackson who was back to polishing glasses.

Jackson watched Abbie walk over to the back till and immediately do what was asked of her.

Something is wrong.

Jackson nudged Eddie as he passed with cut fruit ready for garnish. Jackson gave him a worried look.

"No, I don't think anything feels wrong." He admitted looking about the room. "No one was acting strange last night."

Eddie strolled off, continuing to piece the bar back together.

"Zanahoria?" He started. "Could you fill the ice wells merci!"

Jackson nodded hastily making their way downstairs passing Scott on his way up.

"Hey Al." He approached Ali as she put a collection of steak knives at the far till in preparation for mothers to complain the beef is too tough for their children to cut.

"Abbie sent the coffees down." She tried to guess his complaint.

"No, was just wondering if you had thought anymore about what we were saying last night?" He smiled kindly.

"What we talked about?" She asked in shock and clarification.

"You sounded up for it."

"Chef?" Jasmine's call from the bottom of the stairs pulled his attention back.

"Coming." He called back. " Think about it and let me know." He said to Ali before trotting back down the stairs.

Ali stood holding too many sharp objects looking off into the distance feeling a growing panic fill her.

12:34pm

Danny watched Abbie clearing away the plates of a elderly couple, laughing with them as they made the same joke everyone makes when asked how their food was.

He felt on edge, his stomach was cramped with guilt. Had he ruined it all? What did she feel? He couldn't even decipher what he felt. He had been so content before, life had been simple. A best friend that he got to hang out with every day, a loving girlfriend to go home to. He threw it all away. For what? For her. He still watched her, a small smile flickering on his lips as he remembered what it felt like to be so close, to be with her in a new way.

What is she thinking?

He needed to know. Did she feel it too? What did it mean to her? What did it mean for them?

He looked down and took a breath. Feeling sick with nerves. He had tipped his life on its head, waiting for the pieces to settle back into place. Guilt clenching his empty stomach thinking of Becca. Scared for his friendship with Abbie. What if... he tried to push the thought out of his head... What if it didn't mean anything to her?

What was she thinking?

He looked back up to her, hoping for answers.

Her smile dropped when she turned her back on the customers.

"Don't know why people think telling you their food was awful when they've scraped their plate clean is comedy gold." She tutted dropping the plates on the side ready for him to sort.

"Please can we talk." Danny's words spluttered out before any logic could enter them. He took a few steps around the bar, close to her, close enough she had to tilt her head back slightly to look up at him.

"I'm not sure now is the best time." Abbie stepped back, gesturing to the beginning of Sunday lunch rush filtering into the building.
"I can't focus."
"When do we ever focus?"

"I feel awful. I feel like I've fucked everything up." He carried on. "If I could turn back time."
"Don't bring Cher into this." Abbie rolled her eyes, turning away. He grabbed her arm, pulling her back to look at him. Both his hands rested on her shoulders. She raised her eyebrows nudging him to say his peace. Words formed in his mind but wouldn't push past his mouth. He looked around, unable to hold her stare.
"Come on Danny…" She begged him to say something.

"Becs…" Danny stuttered.
"Don't you think I'm aware you have a girlfriend." Abbie stressed whilst shoving her face into her hands. She took a deep breath which just seemed to be inhaling the smell

of espresso and tobacco which after years in the industry was more like a perfume.

"Daniel!" A voice so sweet just hearing it could give you a toothache. Abbie whipped round to see Rebecca smiling sweetly and making her way over to where they stood awkwardly. Abbie had always thought Rebecca looked impossible, her eyes large and kind as if she had just stepped out of a Pixar movie. Her skin looked airbrushed, and her clothes fell off her as if some invisible being followed her about ensuring the fabric behaved as well as it did on a mannequin. Unfortunately, she was also intelligent and pleasant. Abbie hated that she couldn't hate her. There must have been some Doctor Faustus nonsense happening behind closed doors because Rebecca was impossible.

"Becs!" Danny forced a weary smile. "What are you doing here?" he asked, masking his shock in surprise like a child who had just received an avocado for Christmas.
"Well, we do have a booking."
"We?" He asked stepping past Abbie to approach his girlfriend. She turned to wave at a couple with too few wrinkles which could only be the product of many years of happy marriage. "Mum and Dad are visiting. Remember?"

Danny let Rebecca pull him away. He looked back over his shoulder to throw Abbie an apologetic glance, but she was no longer there.

"Service!" Eddie called out to anyone in earshot. Ali approached, pulling a tray from the pile near where the drinks were dispensed from. "Table 32 please Al."

"Eddie, you didn't happen to overhear anything between me and Scott last night, did you?" She asked carefully whilst pulling the beer and wine onto the tray.

"You guys were talking for a while but it seemed private." he shrugged, already throwing ingredients for the next Bloody Mary into the cocktail shaker.

"Anything at all?" she nudged him. "Any small words? phrases?" She began to lean further over the bar.

"Where to?" Josh asked, pulling the tray of drinks away from Ali.
"32 por favor Josh." Eddie smiled. "Sorry Al, I wish I could help but I'm just not that observant."

Molly turned back to the restaurant. pushing her hands through her hair.

What have I done?

12:50pm

"Abbie." Josie called as she made her way over. Abbie was standing by the till looking out to what was now a sea of happy families.
"Could you take table six's order please." she asked not looking up from the iPad.

"Becca's table?" She clarified. "Can't Ali do it?"

"Well it is in your section." Josie walked away without looking up once.

Abbie pulled out her notepad and pen. She took a deep breath. *Everything is going to be ok. One day we will all laugh about this.*

"Abs?" Ali asked, waving a hand in front of her face.

"I can't do it." She let out a couple heavy breaths.

"I feel you. Yorkshire puddings give me PTSD too."

"No. Yes but no." Abbie sighed. "I can't take Becca's order."

"Oh right. of course." Ali nodded. "I got it."

"Thanks Al." Abbie tried to smile.

"Have you spoken to him?"

"Not really." She looked over to Danny, his back to them both as he made another round of coffees for the chefs. "He said he feels like he fucked up and then started quoting Cher."

Ali rolled her eyes. "You guys need to talk. Make sure you are on the same page."

"I don't think there is a page for this." Abbie started to walk away.

"Oh Ab's." She called her back. "Do you know what I was talking to Scott about last night?"

Abbie scratched her head trying to think back. "I remember you said something about a bit of extra cash."

1:10pm

"Table seven want more gravy." Josh announced whilst logging onto the till.

"Jus not gravy." Danny corrected.
"What's the difference?"

Danny opened his mouth to speak but closed it quickly when he realised he had no idea.
"Josh?" Danny asked and Josh turned around after sending the order "Hypothetically. If you and your…" he trailed off not being able to find the right words. "Wanted to maybe be more than just friends…" he paused again."…but you don't know if they feel the same but maybe it's too risky…maybe it'll all go wrong…but you want to try anyway…but you don't want to hurt anyone… you know? asking for a friend."

"Well, it's all about communication. You gotta make sure you're both thinking the same thing. So, I would tell your hypothetical friend that they should talk to their partner." Josh smiled, enjoying the fact someone was asking him for advice. "It was the same with me and Stevie. I thought we were just joking, having a laugh but turns out he really did think the earth was flat."

Josh finished walking away looking over to Becca sipping her wine. *Poor girl, Danny still thinks you are just friends.*

Danny's confusion was interrupted by the ping of the lift. He opened it up ready to take out the food but all it contained was a single piece of paper reading. ***IT'S JUS!***

1:22pm

Jackson watched the afternoon unfurl. Abbie was working hard, hanging round the back till rather than dispense. Molly looked more confused than normal. Josh hadn't made a single mistake.

Something was definitely wrong.

1:30pm

"Scott!" Ali called as she entered the kitchen. "Table eleven want more gravy."
"It's not gravy, it's jus."

"Table eleven wants more jus."

"We don't have a whole lot and we need to save it for the other roasts."

"Table eleven is Andrew and Leah."

"Means nothing to me." He huffed.

"Lolas parents." Ali elaborated on which the other chefs all smiled letting out short expressions of appreciation for the dog who featured more on the pub's Instagram than any dish on the menu.

"Fine then." He grunted, still plating up a large order of roasts. "I'll send it in the lift."

Ali began to make her way back upstairs, heading toward the lift she passed table eleven assuring them with a smile that they will be able to drown their Yorkshire puddings further at the same time Lola, a tiny white ball of fur jumped up her leg, the dog looked like a cloud wearing a tiny bandana around her neck.

Ali picked up her bottle from next to the coffee machine and filled it with lemonade before waiting by the lift for the jus.

She watched Danny as he repositioned the dirty plates in the bus tray ready to send down to the KP. He purposely didn't look her way, remaining as invested as he could on optimising the space in the deep black tray.

"She told you, didn't she?" He finally said, still not looking up.

"Of course." Ali spoke, sipping her drink.

"What am I supposed to do Al?" He turned to her for answers.

"Be honest." She spoke simply as the lift pinged. As if anything about the situation was simple. Ali pulled the small pot of jus out, squeezing his shoulder before pushing on her best smile ready to be assaulted by the hyper pom pom at table eleven.

Honest? He thought. Becca's musical laugh pulled his attention. She deserved better. but so does Abbie.

Danny suddenly looked up to the speaker as Ed Sheeran filled his ears, to tell him to think out loud. He twisted his head as Jackson put their phone back in their pocket and offered him a small smile, a polishing cloth and a safe space to talk.

1:40pm

Abbie placed the final plate down in front of Becca. "And that's your roast pork, fatty parts cut off." She forced a smile. She felt sick, Becca was so happy. So unaware. Her life might change very soon. Guilt ripped through her stomach making it ache. Part of her wanted to throw up, part of her wanted to confess, get it all out in the open but it wasn't her place. It was Dannys. Abbie's part was done, she had shoved him into a situation sticker than the treacle tart she made with no recipe.

"Thank you, Abigale." She smiled. "You know you should come over sometime."
"I'm sorry?" Abbie was pulled from her rushing thoughts.
"Well Daniel does nothing but talk about you. Maybe you should come by, I mean I feel like we are friends already."
"Sorry I'm busy." Abbie stuttered.
"I'm sure we can get a date in the diary." her smile widened. "Could we get another bottle?" Becca picked up the empty bottle of white from the ice bucket. One that was expensive enough to have a cork not a screw top.

"Of course." Abbie took the bottle from her hand.

"Oh, and some more gravy." Becca called after Abbie as she walked away dazed.

"It's fuckin jus." She groaned under her breath.

2:24pm

"Josie." Ali asked, approaching her as she took off the first round of drinks off table twenty-one who were not happy with the wait on their mains despite being a table of eight who refused to order their mains and starters at the same time.

"What do you need?" Josie acknowledged her whilst she sent down a ticket asking for more gravy.

"Do you know what me and Scott were talking about last night?" She asked hopefully.
"I was pretty absorbed in Candy Crush but thought I heard you mentioning having to do more laundry." She shrugged.
"More laundry?" Ali confirmed, even more confused.

"ITS FUCKING JUS!" Scotts muffled yell managed to reach. Ali and Josie's ears.

"Think he's a bit tired, poor lamb." Josie cooed.

2:38pm

"So how are things?" Becca's father asked, his voice deep but soft.

"Yes, good thank you." Danny wiped his sweaty palms on his jeans. "Same old really, pints to pour, people to serve, food to pronounce wrong." He let out a nervous laugh whilst her mother gave him an encouraging smile that he really was trying his best.

"You have any plans for the future?"

"The future?" Danny stammered.

"You know a period of time which is still to come." He laughed at his own sarcasm which encouraged the others to join.

"Oh yeah. That old chestnut." Danny felt his throat get tight as he looked down to his hands in his lap.

Becca put hers in his and gave it a squeeze. It felt like she had put her hand right into his chest and squeezed his heart, stopping it pumping momentarily.

She doesn't deserve this.

Becca's eyes poured into his own, kind and supportive.

Danny suddenly felt dizzy and grateful to be sat down.

"Well Daniel?" her father pushed, her mother smiled, Becca squeezed.

"I think my immediate future involves me running the dispense section." He gestured to the lift which was being attended to by Jackson. "After that it's anyone's guess." He let out an awkward laugh, carefully pulling his hand away and standing up.

He got back to his position as clanking of the lift stopped, signalling it had reached its peak. He pulled out more roast dinners, plonking them on the side fishing the right ticket off the rail. Josh glanced at the ticket, taking the plates. Danny muttered a thank you after Josh as he walked away, his eyes settling for a moment again on Becca.

It would have been so much easier if things were going wrong, he thought. If they had been fighting. If they had already been having those conversations where they realised they were heading in different directions.

Danny looked away abruptly.

Jackson held out a polishing cloth for him and raised their eyebrows.

"Not right now." He sighed. "I need…" he trailed off whilst shooting for the stairs.

Jackson shrugged, placing it back down onto the side of the bar. Picking up the empty tray and putting it back on top of the dishwasher. They opened it up, steam poured out. After waving it away they took it back to the bar. Ready to carry on. Restarting the cycle. Same movements. Same motions.

Jackson was no longer focusing on the glasses, letting muscle memory take over whilst watching the restaurant.

Sunday lunches were always good for people watching. It was anyone's guess who would show up. Families with more than two generations around one table. Yapping dogs on leads that were a little too long. Every now and again men stopping in for a swift one along their Sunday bike route.

Suddenly the cloth was snatched up. Jackson looked up to Abbie who pulled a pint glass from the tray. Pint glasses didn't particularly need polishing, but they weren't going to mention that now.

"You know, don't you?" She started but continued without pause as she already knew the answer. "Nothing good can start with something bad, can it? Can this situation turn around? Can we pull something out of it?" Abbie sped through the questions. Jackson shrugged with a small nod.

"If I may?" Alec interjected, he moved himself a couple of stools down so that he was now opposite Abbie and Jackson.

"I'll take any wisdom you have today." Abbie smiled, she always liked Alec, he was kind and gentle, he smelt like fudge and kicked Eddie off the top spot of best dressed.
"I found myself in a similar situation when I was a younger lad." he started, swirling his drink a little so the ice spun around the tall glass. "I hadn't been in the service long before I fell for my superior. I was scared of what would happen, she was my boss, our job wasn't really compatible with love either."
"Did you tell her?" Abbie asked, her voice eager.
"I did." He smiled softly, but there was sorrow in it.
"And?"

"She was shot on her next mission." He finished abruptly. "Timing is everything."

Alec shuffled back to his usual seat closer to Eddie's section of the bar.

Abbie and Jackson shared a confused glance, not fully sure what to take from this story.

They both looked over to Becca, letting out a melodic laugh at something her father had said.

"It would be a lot easier if she was a bitch."

2:47pm

"Hey Al" Matteo announced himself as he reached the top of the stairs.

"I'm sorry I tried to tell them they can't have any more Jus."

"Just wanted to pop up in a lull to see if you guys need anything." he stopped her apology in its tracks.

"Oh." Ali said slightly taken aback.

"Weird vibes today." He shivered looking about at the restaurant.

"Hangovers maybe?"

He shuffled slightly closer, leaning against the back wall, dropping closer to her level. "What's the goss?" he whispered with a smile whilst crossing his arms. Mattie let his eyes roam the restaurant, enjoying the natural light spilling in, happy to breathe in air not mingled with sweat.

"No gossip here. We are actually a really boring bunch of people." Ali joked but kept her eyes firmly away from him as she began flipping through her notepad, ripping away orders she no longer needed to hold as evidence.

Mattie snorted and raised an eyebrow in disbelief. He watched as Abbie tripped over the leg of a chair, the single glass on her tray rocking back and forth before deciding to remain upright. He watched Danny wipe the back of his hand along his brow, clocking the t-shirt he let out a small laugh. *They are both taking their job seriously?*

"What's up with Dan and Gail?"

"Nothing." Ali tried to reply casually.

Mattie heard a pleasant tinkling laugh like a bell, he glanced over to where Becca was, it took a moment to place her since the only time they had met was when she came in with a group of her friends to celebrate a promotion and ended up drunk and half asleep on the bar, prosecco still in hand. He saw Danny smile awkwardly in her direction before making himself busy. He saw Abbie switch directions, spotting a single glass on the opposite side of the restaurant.

"Fuck sake." he swore through a deep breath, pulling himself up to full height. "Bloody idiots."

Ali watched his anger rise. she wasn't sure if she had ever seen Mattie angry. In all the years they had worked together. Stressed maybe but never angry.

"Mattie? You alright?" she asked quietly.

He took a deep breath in through his nose.

"I'm fine." He forced an uncomfortable smile before heading back downstairs.

Ali suddenly felt distant, like she no longer knew the people around her.

2:52pm

"Trying to think what to get for my drink." Josh spoke proudly to Abbie, reminding her he lasted all four weeks.

"Whatever you want mate." She smiled, once very glad for Josh's presence.

"Are we allowed top shelf?"

"Anything."

"You know I've never had champagne?" he mused. "Or whiskey." his brows creased a little at realisation he hadn't tried many things.

"Still on Smirnoff ice and apple sours?"

"Last party I went to we actually had VK's I'll have you know, and my mum puts a lot of wine in her Bolognese." he boasted before his smirk fell into a grimace. "God, I'm not ready for uni."

"Have you had a Jager bomb?" She raised her eyebrows.

"I had two on Halloween once."

"You're ready for uni then." he laughed, she mulled over what she was about to say. but recently most things have been against her better judgement so why stop now? "If you ever want to test your limits with someone who has none, you got my number." he smiled gratefully,

174

realising he didn't have her number but would ask for it at a more appropriate time.

Abbie accidentally caught sight of Becca's table; empty plates stacked at the end in effort to help out. She took a deep breath ready to plaster on her best i haven't just slept with your boyfriend smile.

"I got it." Josh strolled past her, already at the table before she could react.

3:13pm

Danny had gone downstairs. He had come down to briefly hide, pretending to table nine he was looking for Dijon mustard even though he knew they only had English left.

Abbie came down the spiral stairs, she slowed down as she clocked him. He looked erratic. Fingers shoved deep into his hair ready to yank it out at the roots.

"Are you ok?" she asked, genuinely concerned. Zero composure suited Danny less than the fedora he tried last autumn.

"I'm going crazy." He admitted. "She's right there. And you are right here. And I wish I was on the fuckin moon, but I can't run away because that's not fair." He pulled his hands out his hair, yesterday's gel still clinging to it made him look like a cartoon drawing with a finger in a plug socket. She wanted to comb his hair down but decided against it. Danny staggered through breaths that were slowly getting shorter. "I just need to think."

"Well whilst you are thinking, I'm going to get a kid an extra Yorkshire pudding he definitely won't be able to eat." Abbie walked around him.

Danny stayed in the corridor. He tried to control his breathing, but it was quick and heavy, his lungs still screamed for air.

Abbie came back past with a lonely Yorkshire pudding on a plate far too big for it.

"Are you mad at me?" He grabbed her arm to spin her back to him. "I'm sorry I've put you in this position. I'm sorry I fucked up. I'm so sorry, it was a big mistake, and it was my fault." Danny pleaded. "Please forgive me." Danny felt panic rise and rise. What could he do? Her face fell along with her shoulders. Her eyes looked deeply into his. Like they had last night, but this time they held hurt.

He felt as if he had pulled a pin and set off a grenade right in the heart of his life. The explosion was going off in slow motion. Abbie, Becca and him. Standing together in the blast zone.

No matter which way he looked there was no way to save them all. Someone was going to be burned, it was inevitable and unstoppable. He wished he could go back. Rewind and stop it from going off.

"I don't want to hurt you." Danny spoke quietly. "I wish I could go back-
"It's ok Danny." She interrupted him and pulled away. "I get it."

Danny watched her walk away. Everything felt wrong. He had never felt so detached from his own life, as if his actions had caused a branch in the fabric of time and he could see himself in a parallel universe where he had turned off the light, locked up, waved goodbye and gone home.

Where he still had his best friend.

3:20pm

"We think we are going to share the plum crumble." Becca smiled at Ali who grinned back unnaturally. Feeling suddenly too hot. They all passed their menus over.

"Sure." She forced a smile, definitely showing too many teeth. "Plum crumble." Ali nervously laughed. "Great choice. Really great choice."

Oh god. play it cool. play it cool. you know nothing. you are not complicit. it's not your place. Deep breaths. you know nothing.

"Was that custard not the ice cream you wanted?" Josh's kind voice broke through Ali's spiral.

"Thank you." Becca smiled sweetly. "I'm Rebecca." She held out her hand to Josh who took it gently shaking it.

"Josh. Pleasure to meet you." He finished before walking away gesturing to Ali to follow. She turned in the opposite direction heading down the stairs. Josh shrugged, plugging the order through the till.

He looked over to Eddie and Jackson working in perfect harmony.

"Do you guys think something feels off today?" he asked, and they both turned in pleasant surprise that he had been the one to start a conversation.

"I'd stay out of it if i were you." Eddie shrugged, turning back to twiddling two bar spoons in two negronis. "Bulls in China shops shouldn't throw stones." Josh's brow creased so he looked to Jackson instead who offered a knowing smirk but shook their head. Josh decided to take their advice, wandering back to Becca's table with dessert spoons, blissfully ignorant.

3:30pm

Danny stood like a deer in headlights by the bar. Frozen stiff by guilt. The lift pinged but he didn't hear. Plates were plopped in front of him, but he didn't notice. His hands were gripping the edge of the bar, right now as if it was the only thing grounding him.

"Danny?" Josh's voice snapped him from his daze. He snapped his head to look at his colleague, a wild look still in his eyes. "The lift is here." He stuttered a little nervously.

"Right." Danny tried to shake himself back into life.

Pulling open the metal doors he sighed. A large portion of honeycomb cheesecake sat well garnished next to a note *for Becca.* He recognised the handwriting as Matts.

"Could you take this over?" Danny passed it to Josh, flashing him the note before dropping it, completely missing the bin at his feet.

"You don't want t-

"I'm busy." He cut him off, reading to resume his position clinging to the bar with everything he had. Josh shuffled off, passing Matt on his way to the table as the chef emerged up the stairs.

Matt stopped in front of Danny, a cigarette balanced behind his ear, his lighter already in his hand.

"You fucked up." Matt said simply, he leaned in closer and put a firm hand on his shoulder. "Give her answers and give her honesty. You can't take back what you did but you can do the right thing now and hope she listens."

Danny took a deep breath, tilting his head back a little in hope to balance the tears forming in his eyes, not wanting them to slip down his face in front of Matt.

"I know." His voice came out strained and raw.

Mattie gave his shoulder a small squeeze before strolling out the front door. Danny watched as he perched on the window sill next to Abbie, he lit his cigarette, even from this distance it was clear the conversation had jumped straight into intense waters.

Danny took a deep breath, knowing right now all he could do was his job, the hard work would come later, and he wouldn't run away.

3:42pm

"Someone must know something right?" Ali stressed, leaning halfway across the bar, but all Jackson could do was shrug whilst twisting a white cloth around a tall glass. "I mean you were drawing people all night. you must have been watching."

Jackson pointed with two fingers to their eyes. "That's true. Watching and listening are different things."

Ali trotted over to the coffee machine, pulling open the drawer underneath it where she had seen Josie stash the napkins from last night. Ali started sifting through Jackson's art, her internal torment giving way to a smile as the memories came back. Christina juggling steak knives. Thomas, Mattie and Carlin making a human pyramid, Danny looking in thought. She grasped at one, holding it taut between her hands. Her and Scott clinking glasses.

"What did you say?" She whispered to the fabric.

"I don't think it will answer." Josh suddenly appeared next to her. She jumped before twisting the napkin toward him.
"Do you know what I was talking about with Scott last night?" her eyes were wild and unblinking.
"I mean I didn't want to eavesdrop, but you mentioned going to hospital." he stuttered, taking a small step away.

"What?" she began checking herself up and down worried.

"I was worried too but you said it was because you are clumsy. So, I assumed it was another long story I shouldn't ask." He decided to shuffle away, not wanting to have survived four weeks just to be murdered at the last hurdle.

4:07pm

"I'll see you later?" Bacca smiled.
"I'm locking up so I might be late."

"Ok darling." She ran her hands through his hair trying to neaten it up.

Abbie watched it all from the other side of the restaurant. He pulled her coat off her chair, holding it out to put it on. Watching her sort out his hair, picking him up and dusting him down. She looked away and blinked back a tear in time for Ali's arm to slide over her shoulders.

"He said it was a mistake, Mols." Her voice turned rough as she suppressed the release of tears. "I know it was. the timing was… but… he thinks it's all a mistake."
"He might not have meant it like that." Ali tried to comfort her friend.
"Why would he choose me? over her?" her thoughts carried on. "We are better off as friends."
"Can you be?"
"Friends again?" Abbie watched Becca lean up and kiss his cheek. She felt a stab in her chest. Guilt, pain or jealousy. she wasn't sure. "I don't know."

Danny smiled sadly as Becca kissed his cheek. He felt shame in it. He had betrayed her.

"Hey Bec?" He spoke softly. "Maybe tomorrow, could I talk to you?"

"You don't need to ask." She smiled, oblivious. "Is something wrong?"

"I just got some stuff I need to get off my chest."

She gave him another sweet smile and he tried to smile back as he watched her leave happily with her parents in tow.

4:35pm

The main rush was over. Ali deposited a load of empty glasses on the end of the bar and turned back to the restaurant. It was still full, but most were finishing desserts, she was waiting patiently to see people making little check signs in the air.

Scott made his way upstairs and over to her. *Private. More laundry. More money. Hospital trips.*

"Don't worry if you need more time but just wanted to check what your thoughts were?" he smiled.
"Well, I'll be honest-

"We would love to have you down in the kitchen." His tone was supportive and kind. "I just thought while you are figuring out your long-term goal, might be a good place to get some new skills, new experience. Carlin wants to cut his hours back a bit. Could get you part time down there, part time up here for a bit. Just a trial. See how you feel."

"Wow." she was taken aback.

"I know you had your reservations. I mean we are all a little clumsy but honestly the food stains come out easier than you think."
She let out a deep breath of relief as it all fell into place.

"Take your time thinking." Scott said patiently. Ali was ready to start her list of pros and cons, but her gut took over.

"That sounds pretty good actually."
"Amazing." he grinned. "I'll talk to Josie."

5:10pm

Danny wandered round the bar. Picking up a polishing cloth and a hot steaming wine glass. Jackson looked up to him expectantly.

"I think I've fucked it." He began. "It shouldn't have happened like this." Jackson listened patiently, letting his thoughts flow. "I think deep down I've known I've wanted her for a long time. Spending time with her is all I look forward to. When I make her laugh it is one of the best feelings. I just didn't think she felt the same way."

"You're fuckin joking!" Eddie's voice interrupted from the other side of the bar. Danny and Jackson looked over with raised eyebrows. "pardonne-moi." he took his focus back to his cocktail.

"I've gone about this all wrong. It was a mistake to do it the way we did." Danny sighed. "But it was the best mistake I've ever made."

7:40pm

"Danny." Ali called to him as he scraped a half-eaten roast dinner into the bin. "Josie wants you in the office."

He wiped his fingers on the tea towel tucked into his back pocket, dragging himself down the spiral stairs.

"You ok Jose?" He asked, leaning in the doorway to the office.

"Yes." She said brightly. "Just wanted to have a little catch up quick."
"Sure."
"So we need to put up an ad for waiting staff tomorrow. Just need to make sure you are checking through and printing off CVs of the good applicants."
"I thought Al was just having a trial in the kitchen, you know doing the lunches to see how she feels?"
"Yes, she is but this is for Abbie's replacement."
"What?" Danny felt as if the carpet had suddenly torn from underneath him.
"I'm sorry I thought you already knew. She is taking a leave of absence." Josie said, alarmed at his surprise. They looked at each other blankly. neither knowing what to say. Josie blinked and stood up. "I'm just going to discuss some things with Scott but if you could be on top of that this week, I would appreciate it." she finished edging past him carefully, as if even brushing him he would crumble.

Danny pounded up the stairs and tore outside where Abbie was leaning against the side of the window. She took another drag of her cigarette as he approached fast.

"You're leaving?" Danny asked, still in disbelief. "Just like that?"

"No, I've got a notice period." she said. "Anyway, it's just a leave of absence, whilst I figure things out."

"You'll come back?" Danny's question came out as a plea. She looked down to the floor, leaving the question in the space between them. "I'm sorry Abbie. you know i am."

"I know Danny." she sighed. "And I'm sorry too."

"You can't leave." He begged. "This place is nothing without you."
"It'll be exactly the same."
"Not for me." he spoke fast. "Abs-

"What am I supposed to do? Sit around and wait for you?"

"Now who's bringing Cher into this." He tried to joke but she crossed her arms.

"Danny. I've made up my mind. I've been putting my life off for too long." She said defiantly but refused to look at him.

She flicked her cigarette to the ground and walked past him.

"Abs." He pulled her attention back. Finally finding the words he had been hunting for all day. "I don't regret it."

She glanced at him over her shoulder.

"Neither do I."

The door shut and Danny was left alone under the street-light. The sign to the Bells swayed gently above his head.

8:00pm

"There you have it." Eddie laid it in front. "Try and enjoy it." He grimaced slightly before walking away. A tall glass of champagne, mixed with top shelf whiskey. Josh watched the lone strawberry garnish float, bubbles cling-ing to its edges. *Victory.*

"Hey Abbie." Josh raised his glass to her as she reached the top of the stairs with her bag.

"Congratulations." She smiled flatly walking over. Sud-denly his win didn't taste so sweet. If he had taken a sip yet he would realise champagne and whisky didn't taste sweet in the slightest.

"You should have it." Josh pushed the drink toward her.

Abbie smiled sincerely but shook her head.

"Appreciate the gesture but I know when I'm beat. It's all yours."

She turned to leave.

"Not staying for a drink?" Thomas called to her as he dropped his bag by a bar stool picking up his pint.

"Nah not tonight." She shrugged casually.

"Fair enough." he sat himself down next to Josh.

Abbie lingered at the door, looking past them both to Danny who was wiping down his section. He looked tired, his hair flat, his t-shirt dirty, his shoulders slumped. She turned away, pushing through the door.

Danny looked up, watching her leave. Wondering if he ran out would it change anything.

A gentle guitar came over the speakers.

Danny looked over to Jackson who offered a sympathetic smile, putting their phone back away.

He watched through the window as she walked off.

"Only know you love her when you let her go. and you let her go."

Saturday. 5:30pm

"Excuse me?" Clemmie asked as confidently as possible. "I'm looking for Josie."

"You must be Clemmie!" Josie grinned, stepping to the side to let the girl enter. She was young, short brown choppy hair littered with streaks of colour subtly inter-woven. She had worn black shirt and loose black trousers, even polished her black boots.

She followed Josie to the end of the bar where a boy was standing by a coffee machine, steaming milk which made a satisfying hiss as it heated in the jug.

"Josh?" Josie called for his attention. "Can you show Clemmie around please."

Josie strolled off casually tapping at her iPad. Clemmie looked at the boy, his trainers were scuffed, baggy trousers and uncombed curly hair.

Only when he finished making his drink did he turn round to address her.

He had a bright smile; his t-shirt had some equation on it with the words *no flux given* underneath it.

"Hi I'm Josh." He sipped his hot chocolate. "Welcome to the Bells."